"You c... of thing often?"

"No," Helen snapped at Jay's taunting remark. "And it wasn't my idea. I can explain."

"Good," Jay tossed back, "because the last thing I remember is being in a garden with a particularly beautiful woman, and then I wake up here doped to the eyeballs. I do take it I've been kidnapped?"

"Sort of," Helen managed to get out, her nerves positively frayed by the little Jay did remember.

"And what possible motive could you have for holding me here, Helen?"

"You remember my name?" she gulped.

"Helen," Jay said, his tone brusque, "there are plenty of things about last night that are hazy, but you're not one of them."

Kate Walker chose the Brontë sisters, the development of their writing from childhood to maturity, as the topic for her master's thesis. It is little wonder, then, that she should go on to write romance fiction. She lives in the United Kingdom with her husband and son, and when she isn't writing, she tries to keep up with her hobbies of embroidery, knitting, antiques and, of course, reading.

Don't miss any of our special offers. Write to us at the following address for information on our newest releases.

Harlequin Reader Service
901 Fuhrmann Blvd., P.O. Box 1397, Buffalo, NY 14240
Canadian address: P.O. Box 603,
Fort Erie, Ont. L2A 5X3

Captive
Lover
Kate Walker

Harlequin Books

TORONTO • NEW YORK • LONDON
AMSTERDAM • PARIS • SYDNEY • HAMBURG
STOCKHOLM • ATHENS • TOKYO • MILAN

Original hardcover edition published in 1987
by Mills & Boon Limited

ISBN 0-373-02910-1

Harlequin Romance first edition May 1988
Second printing May 1988

For Julie and Richard

CHAPTER ONE

'KIDNAP him!' Helen's voice was sharp with disbelief. 'I don't believe you. Ricky, you can't be serious.'

'Never more so.' Richard Seymour's face broke into a wide, gleeful grin at the sight of his sister's discomfiture. 'The committee asked me to come up with a good idea, and you've got to admit that this one's a stunner.'

'You can say that again,' Helen declared emphatically. Stunned was an understatement for the way she was feeling. Her mind seemed to have stopped working; it was as if someone had thumped her over the head with an iron bar. 'But—isn't it illegal? What about the police?' she managed unsteadily.

'Oh, there'll be no bother with them.' Ricky dismissed her objections airily. 'After all, it's not as if we're going to harm him. It's just a publicity stunt, and if I know Jay Keller he'll do anything for a bit of free press exposure. He thrives on it. Come on, Nell,' he added persuasively, 'look on the positive side. We need a stunt that will draw attention to what we're doing and, hopefully, boost our funds—and Keller can certainly do that. He's loaded, absolutely rolling in money, so he won't miss a small contribution.'

That Helen wasn't disputing. It was well known that rock star Jay Keller was one of the richest men in the country. He could certainly afford to give away a year's income and not even notice, and if Ricky could get him

7

to contribute to their campaign then she was all for it—
but it was the method her brother had decided on of
getting Keller to contribute that worried her.

'But can't you just ask him for a donation?'

'Oh, come off it, Nell, where's the fun in that? This is
Rag Week we're talking about—madness and may-
hem—no holds barred. The more outrageous the stunt
the better. A straightforward donation would be too
boring and it wouldn't give us the press coverage we
need, surely you can see that.'

She could, of course, but Helen still wasn't happy
about things. But she didn't get a chance to voice any
further objections because at that moment Ricky took
her breath away by adding cajolingly, 'Please, Sis, loosen
up a bit. It's just a bit of fun—no harm in it—and all in a
very good cause. I've got it all planned out, but I can't do
it unless you help.'

'*Me?*' Helen had thought it was impossible to feel any
more shock, but her brother's last comment made her
head reel. 'Me?' she repeated, pushing a hand through
her long black hair in a gesture of exasperation. 'What
can I do, Ricky? I'm not even at the Poly and——'

'I know.' Ricky cut in on her spluttered protests. 'But
that's exactly why you *can* help. We'll have to put Keller
somewhere when we've got him, and all the other guys
who're in on this live in digs or a hall of residence—we
can't possibly hide him there—so——'

The bewildered look on Helen's face changed swiftly
to one of incredulous comprehension.

'You want to bring him *here*! That *is* what you're trying
to say, isn't it?'

Ricky nodded smilingly. 'This house would be just
perfect. There's the spare room going begging, and it's

far enough out of the town centre not to attract attention
and——'

'*No!*'

Helen's tone was vehement. When she had agreed to
let her younger brother come and lodge with her when he
had started his course at the Polytechnic, she had
accepted the fact that for a few years at least her house
wouldn't be the peaceful home she was used to. She had
anticipated friends calling in at all hours of the day and
night, a few noisy parties perhaps, and those she had
been prepared to tolerate—but this was something
completely different.

'Definitely not,' she said even more firmly. 'If you're
determined to go through with this crazy idea, Ricky,
then, short of locking you in your bedroom, I don't
suppose I can do anything to stop you. But I don't
approve and I will not be dragged into it with you.'

'Lord, Nell, anyone would think I'd suggested assas-
sinating the fellow!' Ricky's face had fallen despondently. 'Can't you see it's just going to be a rag stunt—no one's
going to get hurt, except perhaps Keller's bank balance,
and he can spare the odd hundred or two without even
blinking. And I'm sure Keller himself would go along
with it,' he added persuasively. 'He's only coming to a
backwoods place like this because it's for charity and
because he was a student here himself once—years ago—
so he'll remember what Rag Week's like. Look, all we
need is a bed and some food for him until we've sorted
out the financial side of things—and you did say you
wanted to help with the campaign.'

Helen was finding it a struggle to resist the pleading
look on her brother's face, a struggle that she abandoned
when she heard his next remark.

'Think about Trish,' Ricky said, 'and how much all this would have meant to her.'

Helen's grey eyes clouded. 'That, brother dear, was definitely below the belt' she said, remembered pain making her voice tart, all the more so because she could not deny the effectiveness of the weapon Ricky was using against her. Even after six years, the memory of the death of her young sister from kidney failure was almost more than she could bear.

'Was it?' Ricky questioned softly. 'Do you want other kids to suffer as she did? If we can save just one life as a result of our fund-raising, doesn't that justify anything we do?'

'Not *anything*.' But Helen's voice did not have quite the conviction she wanted. Ricky knew he had touched a raw spot and pressed home his advantage mercilessly.

'Just think what a difference it could have made if the Kidney Unit had been expanded when Trish was alive. She might have had a chance then. Well, it's too late for Trish now, but at least other kids can be helped—but they need every penny they can get and that's where we come in. I had the devil of a fight to get the Rag Committee to agree to donate all the money we raise to the Kidney Unit's appeal fund, everyone had their own pet charity they wanted to support, but I did persuade them—and now I'm going to make damn sure this is the best Rag the Poly's ever had so that the unit can benefit to the fullest possible extent.'

Helen could not suppress the small smile that crossed her lips at the sight of her brother's enthusiasm. If determination and hard work meant anything, then she knew he would succeed in his aims. Ricky had changed a lot in the eight months since he had first come to live with her; she had watched the uncertain, rather gauche adolescent become a confident, independent person. The Ricky of twenty had come a long way from the desolate boy of fourteen who had been shattered by the death of a sister only two years younger than himself.

Remembering those dark days, Helen thought she understood just why Ricky was determined to go ahead with his madcap scheme. If Trish had still been alive, if a much-needed injection of cash for dialysis machines or transplant surgery might have saved her sister, would she still have hesitated? Helen was forced to question herself, knowing even as the doubt formed in her thoughts that if that had been the case then, like Ricky, she would have felt that the end justified any means. So why should it make any difference because it was some other child, or an adult, who could be saved by their actions?

'What do you want me to do?' she asked slowly.

Helen pulled open her wardrobe door and surveyed its contents uncertainly. Just what did one wear to a kidnapping? she thought slightly hysterically, wishing, not for the first time, that she had stuck to her guns and refused to go along with Ricky's crazy idea. She had managed to suppress her misgivings enough to agree to having Jay Keller in the house overnight while the 'ransom' was negotiated.

'It'll only be for one night,' Ricky had assured her. 'Twenty-four hours at the most—I promise.'

But her doubts had revived again when her brother had added the request that she let them use her car to transport Keller to her home and, finally, that she came along herself.

'Why do I have to be there?' she exploded. 'You said you had it all worked out between you—you didn't need my help. I don't want to be involved with that side of things!'

'But you are involved,' Ricky pointed out. 'You were involved from the minute you said you'd have him here, You aren't going to back out now, are you? The concert's only two days away.'

'No,' Helen sighed. She had given her word and she wasn't someone who went back on a promise. 'No, I'm not going to back out—but I just don't see why you need me to be there when you——' Her voice faltered, she found herself unable to form the words 'kidnap him'.

'Do the deed?' Ricky supplied cheerfully, his eyes sparkling with barely suppressed excitement. 'Oh, come on, Nell, you wouldn't want to miss out on that, would you?'

'I most definitely would!' Helen's tone was sharp. If she could, she would willingly miss out on all of this, but she had committed herself now, there was no going back.

'But we need you,' Ricky continued unabashed. 'Someone has to distract Keller, occupy his attention while we get organised, and that someone has to be female. We know he's got an eye for the ladies, particularly tall, raven-haired beauties, and you fit that description perfectly.'

'So does Sarah!' Helen retorted, not in the least swayed by her brother's blatant flattery. Without vanity she knew that her fresh, flawless complexion, full mouth and widely spaced, soft grey eyes, when combined with her slender height and jet-black hair, gave her an appearance that had attracted many men in the past, but the events of that spring day a year before had left her unable to give any credence to terms such a 'beautiful' when applied to herself. 'She's as tall and dark as I am. Why can't your girlfriend do the "distracting"?'

'Sarah's not going to the concert.' Ricky dismissed Helen's objection with a wave of his hand. 'She's in the play the Drama Group's putting on all week, so it has to be you. Besides, I think it will be good for you. It's time you got out into circulation again. You can't hide away with a broken heart for ever.'

'I'm not hiding!' Helen snapped, the flippancy of that 'broken heart' stinging more than she was prepared to let Ricky see. It was just a year since the day that should have been her wedding day, a year in which she had slowly and painfully picked up the pieces of her life and had begun to look forward to a different future from the one that had been shattered by the arrival of a telegram only an hour before the marriage ceremony. But underneath the fragile scars the wounds were still raw and Ricky's dig had probed too deeply. 'I'm perfectly happy the way I am!'

Ricky looked sceptical. 'Do you expect me to believe that?' he demanded. 'When did you last have any *fun*? You're twenty-five, not ninety-five, and most women would pay a fortune for a chance to go to a Jay Keller concert.'

'I don't like rock music!' Helen protested unevenly. It was a long time since the determination she had so admired in her brother had been used against her and she was uncomfortably aware of the way she was being backed into a corner.

'You can't not like Keller's stuff!' Ricky was openly incredulous. 'He's the greatest—the best ever! OK,' he continued more quietly, seeing that Helen was unconvinced. 'So his music's not to your taste, but what about the man himself? What about meeting the sex symbol of the century? Think about it, Nell.'

Think about it! Helen almost laughed out loud. She had done nothing but think about it ever since Ricky had first come up with his hare-brained scheme. A vivid picture floated before her eyes, the image of Jay Keller seen on innumerable television shows, his strong, lithe body clothed in some blatantly flamboyant outfit like the skin-tight black leather trousers and clinging red silk T-shirt he had worn on the latest spectacular, the shirt cut deliberately low to reveal the tiny butterfly tattoo at the base of his throat, its delicacy startling against the firm muscle.

Helen hated tattoos, finding them unnatural and physically repellent, and she had never been impressed by Keller's stage act either, though she knew there were plenty who found it the most wonderful thing since sliced bread. Only the week before, Keller had appeared on the weekly chart show, performing his latest hit record which had been at number one for six weeks now, and Helen had watched as, with his tousled mane of golden hair gleaming in the spotlight and the sweat pouring down his face, he had strutted and swayed through the number.

How obvious! Helen had thought cynically, not deceived for a moment by such deliberate showmanship, and now, recalling those scenes, the hysteria of the fans that surrounded Keller and the way their screams had clearly fed the ego of the singer, she felt suddenly cold at the realisation that *this* was the man she had agreed to let stay in her home, and she was very thankful that at least Ricky would be there too.

'All right, you don't have to come to the concert,' Ricky was saying. 'But we do need you later. We're all meeting for drinks after the show—and that's when we go into action. So say you'll come, Helen, *please!*'

Helen had opened her mouth to utter an adamant refusal when, clearly reading her intention in her eyes, Ricky added quietly, 'For Trish's sake,' once more using the weapon against which she had no defence, and in a second her 'No' had been transformed into a slow and reluctant 'Yes'.

Which was why she was standing here staring blankly at the array of clothes before her, wondering just what she was going to wear.

Helen gave herself a small shake. The concert finished at ten, she would have to get to the Polytechnic at least a quarter of an hour before that or she would become engulfed in the crowds of fans leaving the hall, and it was already well after eight. She had better hurry up and decide or it would be too late.

Almost two hours later she was beginning to wish she *had* left it too late. If she had been caught up in the crowds she would have had some sort of an excuse for giving up and going home, leaving Ricky and his friends to carry on without her. Instead of which she was crammed into a corner of the noisy, crowded bar, a glass of wine she wasn't enjoying in one hand and the beginnings of a tension headache lurking painfully around her temples—and she had been here half an hour or more without one single sight of the famous Mr Keller.

She *had* seen Ricky, though. He had bounded up to her

on her arrival, blue eyes gleaming, lips pursed into a teasing wolf-whistle at the sight of her tall, slender form in the dark red silk trousers and white lace blouse she had finally chosen.

'You look stunning, Sis!' he had exclaimed. 'That outfit is really something! You never used to dress like that.'

Helen's wry smile acknowledged the truth of his statement. David had hated women in trousers and, to please him, she had never worn them, in spite of the fact that her slender hips and long legs were eminently suited to such a style. But David wasn't part of her life any more and one of the small pleasures she had rediscovered since his jilting of her was that of being able to wear what she liked. He had preferred her to wear her long jet-black hair up too, not hanging loose in a soft, waving mane as she wore it now.

The smile wavered slightly. Helen didn't want to think of David now. Her stomach was knotted tight with tension as it was, and she couldn't risk letting her thoughts wander off down a path that might weaken her resolve. With a determined effort she switched the smile back on, lifting her head in a gesture that sent her dark silky hair flying.

'If I'm supposed to play the *femme fatale* I thought I'd better look the part,' she laughed, almost convincingly, but the smile she had managed didn't quite reach her almond-shaped, soft grey eyes. 'So where's the famous superstar? I don't see your sexy Mr Keller anywhere.'

'He's signing autographs,' Ricky told her. 'That'll keep him tied up for a while. He's always willing to give his fans plenty of time.'

'I see.' Helen frowned thoughtfully as she notched up

an unexpected point in Jay Keller's favour. After seeing the blatantly manipulative way he had enticed and seduced his audience on the television show, she had been inclined to suspect that he would have an equally pragmatic attitude to them when off-stage, and she found herself pleasantly surprised to discover that this was not in fact the case. It was just a small thing, but nevertheless it made her feel one degree better about Jay Keller spending the night in her home.

But now, in her cramped corner, oppressed by the heat and the smoky atmosphere, Helen could have wished that Jay Keller had been slightly less concerned about his fans. She knew no one in the room, they were all students at the Polytechnic, nearer Ricky's age than her own, and as her brother and his friends had disappeared heaven knew where she was completely alone. For the last five minutes she had been watching the second-hand on the large wall clock move slowly round, her tension growing with every second that ticked away. Ricky's instructions had been simple, to him at least. She was to manoeuvre herself close to Jay Keller, strike up a conversation, and then somehow draw him out of the room and into the garden where Ricky and Co. would be waiting.

It was that 'somehow' that worried her. Just what excuse could she give for taking Jay Keller away from this party, a party given solely for his benefit, and could she really play her part without giving herself away? Helen's grey eyes clouded and she bit her lower lip nervously. Just to think of it made her throat so dry she doubted she would be able to speak a word. Her eyes smarted in the smoke from a cigarette carelessly brandished by a woman who stood nearby and she blinked them hard to ease the sensation then, opening them again, froze, her hand clenching on her glass. In the second she had had her eyes closed her brother had appeared from nowhere and there was no mistaking the identity of the man at his side. The glorious colour of his hair gave him away immediately, in spite of the fact that the wild, unruly mane of the television performance had been ruthlessly suppressed so that his hair now lay sleek and smooth against his well shaped head. He was Jay Keller all right—and he was heading straight towards her!

'I'd like you to meet my sister, Helen.'

Helen heard Ricky's words through a pounding like the noise of distant thunder which she suddenly realised was the sound of her own heart thudding unnaturally swiftly, setting the blood racing through her veins so that she missed Jay Keller's politely formal greeting, the haze in her mind clearing only as he released the hand she had automatically held out to him and which he had taken in a firm, warm grasp.

'It's a pleasure to meet you, Mr Keller,' she managed stumblingly, her mind too numb to think up anything more, though she didn't need Ricky's faint frown to tell her that this was hardly the way to start the scintillating sort of conversation that was supposed to entice Jay Keller out into the garden with her.

'Jay, please,' he said easily, the pleasant smoothness of his voice soothing her ruffled nerves so that, after a surreptitious deep breath and a hasty swallow to ease her still dry throat, she finally managed to focus her eyes on him.

Jay Keller's appearance was in sharp contrast to the flamboyant creature she had expected from seeing him on the television show, and it wasn't just the smooth hair that made the difference. He was sharply elegant in a crisp white suit and black silk shirt, the immaculately tailored clothes sitting perfectly on a frame that was slim but well muscled. He had looked taller on television, Helen thought, but perhaps that was jut the contrast with Ricky's well built height. Either way, the two-inch heels on her shoes made it easy for her to meet his eyes—and what eyes! Jewel-bright, emerald green, and framed by the thickest lashes she had ever seen, they had a powerfully arresting quality when contrasted with the clean, firm lines of his facial bones.

Seeing those eyes fixed firmly on her face, Helen's heart quailed inside her. That sharp, green gaze had already missed nothing of her discomposure. She was going to have to work very hard if she was to pull off this pretence with any degree of success.

'Are you a student too, Miss Seymour?' Jay was asking, and Helen shook her head.

'No, I work for a local estate agent—Frazer and Crown. My official title is personal assistant to Mr Crown but that usually means I end up as general dogsbody, answering the phone, writing letters, and very often showing prospective buyers round houses.'

This was better, she had brought a slight smile to that firm mouth, and she noticed that Ricky had relaxed perceptibly.

'Nell could sell an igloo in the Sahara,' he put in now. 'Frazer and Crown haven't looked back since they took her on. Can I get you a drink, Jay? You must need one after two hours on stage. What about you, Sis?'

'Not for me, thanks.' Helen lifted her still half-full glass. She couldn't take any risks, she needed a clear head for what was coming. On that thought she glanced at Jay

Keller again and her heart seemed to turn over inside her at the thought that in a very short time this man would be installed in her spare bedroom, kept there against his will.

Covertly she studied him from under lowered eyelids, wondering how he would react. Would he be angry or would he, as Ricky had so often assured her, simply take it all as a joke, a bit of fun and a welcome dose of publicity? She couldn't judge. That firm-boned face was a mystery to her, its features formed into an expression of polite interest, but those bright, clear eyes wandered over the faces of the crowd with a rather aloof, almost distant look in them. Was he bored? Helen wondered. Very likely, he had probably attended hundreds of such functions in his years at the top. He was something of a phenomenon really, a man who had had his first hit ten years ago and who, even at the age of thirty-two, could still attract a teenage audience.

'So did you enjoy the all-singing, all-dancing, never-standing-still Jay Keller spectacular?' Jay Keller's low, pleasant voice broke in on her thoughts, the unexpected note of cynicism in it shocking her into complete honesty.

'I didn't see the concert.' Or was that the wrong thing to say? Hastily she softened her comment by adding, 'The tickets were sold out in two days.'

Jay's slight smile was disturbing, she didn't quite know how to interpret it.

'And do you come to many student functions?'

'Not really—hardly at all, in fact.'

'So why this one?'

Was he fishing for compliments? Helen wondered. Did he want her to say that, like those others Ricky had described, she would have sold her soul to meet the great

Jay Keller? Didn't he have enough flatterers and hangers-on ready to feed his ego at the slightest encouragement?

'Ricky invited me,' she said stiffly, aiming for a deliberate put-down.

Jay Keller appeared unconcerned. Not by the faintest flicker of a response did he reveal whether he had sensed the point of her remark.

'And do you always go where your younger brother takes you?'

A strange question, and one she wasn't quite sure how to answer. 'I don't know what you mean.'

'I was just curious.' A wave of one hand indicated the crowded room. 'You don't seem to fit in somehow. You're not at all like most of the women here.'

A quick survey of the females nearest them confirmed Jay's remark. Not one of them was over twenty and they were all dressed in the latest and wildest of fashions with bright clashing colours and heavy junk jewellery, making the restrained elegance of her own clothes stand out sharply in contrast. A feeling like the cold prick of pins and needles ran through Helen's veins. Was Keller becoming suspicious? Did he have some sense that she was here for reasons other than the most obvious ones?

'Well, of course this is a very different occasion.'

'And why's that?'

A swift glance into those emerald eyes told Helen that she had been wrong when she had suspected that Jay Keller was fishing for compliments. His gaze was clear and open and revealed only a genuine interest in the answer to his question. He was interested in *her*; he wasn't trying to make her say something about himself.

The realisation that she had succeeded at least in part

of the plan that Ricky had outlined should have brought
some sense of relaxation, but, surprisingly, it had just the
opposite effect. David's desertion had hurt her so
savagely that since the day he had jilted her she had
carefully avoided any situation that might lay her open to
such pain again. It was a long time since she had seen
that spark of interest in a man's eyes, and to find that it
was there now, in the face of this man whom she was
deliberately deceiving, shattered her composure. Her lips
were painfully dry and she wetted them nervously with
her tongue, seeing those vivid eyes flick downwards to
follow the slight movement.

'It's Rag Week,' she managed clumsily. 'And that's a
special time. Everyone joins in to make the events a
success. Most of the time the students and the town keep
themselves quite separate, but in Rag Week everyone
comes together and works to help other people. And of
course it's for such an important cause. All the proceeds
from this week are going to support the hospital's Kidney
Unit. If we can buy even one new dialysis machine it will
be something. There are so many people suffering from
kidney disease, so many children without a hope of a
decent life if we don't help them.'

Her tongue had run away with her, she realised on a
wave of embarrassment as she caught the faintly
bemused look that crossed Jay Keller's features in the
face of her sudden vehemence. Was it really just her own
deeply felt enthusiasm that had made her so eloquent, or
was she preparing the ground, laying down defences
against the moment when Keller knew, as he inevitably
must know sooner or later, exactly what she was doing
here? If she convinced him of the rightness of their cause,

then surely he would take their plans for him in good part?

'You're very committed to the whole idea,' he said now. 'Obviously you feel very strongly about it.'

'Oh, I do.' Helen grasped at the straw of a subject she could talk about honestly and without restraint. 'I just wish I could do more to help. I carry a donor card, of course, but——'

Her voice faltered on the last words and then failed her completely. For years now she had carried the little red and blue kidney donor card with her everywhere she went. It was in her handbag now, tucked inside her purse. But when it had mattered most, when she would willingly have given one of her own kidneys to save her little sister, it had been impossible.

She knew the colour had left her cheeks, and saw concern suddenly darken Keller's eyes as he noticed her pallor.

'Are you all right?'

'I—it's just a headache.' And that at least was the truth. The tension in the muscles at the back of her neck had revived the headache that had been threatening earlier, making her head pound painfully.

At that moment, Ricky appeared with the drinks, taking in the situation at a glance.

'Perhaps you'd feel better with some fresh air.' He was quick to seize on the opportunity she had so unthinkingly given him. 'It is terribly smoky in here. Why don't you take her out into the garden, Jay? I'll just——'

He moved away without even bothering to think up some excuse for his departure. Damn you, Ricky! Helen thought hazily. Couldn't you have stayed to help? I don't know if I can manage this on my own.

But it was too late for second thoughts. Already Jay had slipped a hand under her elbow and was guiding her carefully towards the door that opened on to the garden, fending off anyone who tried to gain his attention with a polite but firm determination. The touch of his fingers on her arm made Helen shiver in reaction, and she could only hope that Jay interpreted her response as being to the cool night air that hit them as soon as they stepped outside.

'Here, sit down.' Jay's voice was solicitous as he led her towards a wooden bench that stood on the crisp, short grass. Helen sank on to it thankfully, leaning back against its firm support and closing her eyes with a sigh of relief. It had been very smoky and warm inside the bar. She drew in slow, deep breaths of the night air, feeling its coolness soothe her and ease the painful racing of her heart. 'Better now?' Jay asked.

Helen nodded and managed to find her voice. 'Much better, thanks. I don't usually go faint like that; I don't know what came over me.'

But deep down she *did* know what had happened. It wasn't just her memories of Trish that had upset her. The sense of unreality that had gripped her all evening had expanded in her brain, pervading every nerve until she felt she was living through some crazy dream—or rather nightmare—one in which none of the small realities that kept her sane existed. How could she ever have let herself get caught up in plans to kidnap and hold to ransom another human being, however light-heartedly and for whatever reason? This couldn't be happening! It just wasn't true!

But even as the thoughts filled her head Jay lowered himself on to the bench beside her, the warmth of his body so close to hers reaching her through the thin material of her blouse, his thigh almost touching hers as he stretched his long legs out in front of him, and she knew with a jolting shock that it *was* real, it *was* happening and that now she was on the merry-go-round she couldn't get off. Without quite knowing how it had happened she now found she had moved on to the second stage of Ricky's plan. Just as her brother had wanted, she had brought Jay out of the bar and into the garden—but what happened next? Ricky had held his cards very close to his chest when it came to revealing any details of what he and his friends planned to do. Just *how* were they going to manage the actual kidnapping?

Helen's eyes flew open to focus on the man at her side, his white jacket and trousers etched sharply against the darkness of evening, but with his face hidden in shadow as he drained the last of his drink from the glass he had brought out with him. Sitting so close to him, she couldn't be unaware of the fact that, for all it was not so bulky as Ricky's, Jay's firmly muscled body had a compact strength that could make him a formidable opponent if it came to a struggle.

The knots of tension in her stomach tightened painfully at the thought. What *did* Ricky plan to do? She couldn't see Jay Keller simply agreeing to get into the car and drive away with them, and if there was a fight it would defeat all their plans by attracting the sort of attention they didn't want. If there was a fight! Helen shuddered faintly at the prospect.

'Do you feel like talking?' Jay's quiet voice reached her on the still night air, jolting her back to reality with a jerk.

'Oh yes, I feel fine now.' For all she had worked hard on pitching her voice at a relaxed and carefree level, she hadn't quite succeeded; the words came out unevenly and she sounded breathless. Fixing her eyes on the horizon and the moon which had risen, clear and bright and perfectly round, Helen tried again. 'The sky's very clear tonight, isn't it? You can see all the stars perfectly.'

Jay's wordless murmur might have been one of agreement, at least Helen determined to take it as such.

'And the moon's so beautiful, so still and serene.' Oh dear, this didn't sound at all right. Her voice gave away too much and the inanities she was speaking only aggravated the problem. 'Don't you find it hard to believe that man has actually set foot up there? It seems impossible, doesn't it? Seen like this the moon looks so pure and virginal—it just *has* to be female, never mind the man in the——'

'Why are you so jumpy?' The question came with a disconcerting suddenness, breaking into her words and leaving her floundering.

'I don't—I mean—am I?' Helen's heart sank as she caught Jay's quick frown and knew she had only made matters worse.

'I think you've just proved my point,' he murmured. 'What is it? There may be a full moon out but I'm no werewolf—look——'

He held his hands out towards her, the strong, square-tipped fingers spread wide, then, as Helen stared in blank confusion, he grinned and explained.

'Don't you know the legend? It's said that a true werewolf has the fourth finger longer than the third on each hand—but I don't. See?'

He lifted his hands again to prove his point, the smile spreading over his face to reveal very white teeth. His grin was infectious and Helen felt her own lips curve in response.

'So you're not a werewolf,' she said lightly. 'And not, I hope, a vampire either?'

Still smiling, Jay shook his head. 'Nothing so bloodthirsty,' he laughed. 'I'm a very ordinary human being.' Abruptly his expression sobered. 'But the full moon is having an effect on me—at least the way its light falls on your face is. You're very beautiful, Helen, in fact you're quite the loveliest woman I've ever seen. I want to get to know you—to learn everything about you.'

'You—I——' Helen spluttered incoherently, panic overwhelming her. His words alone were enough to raise bitter memories, but uppermost in her mind was the thought that this was a complication she hadn't anticipated. Ricky had told her that Keller liked tall, dark-haired girls, but she had never expected him to take matters quite this far!

Looking back, she saw how she had fooled herself by believing that *she* had had anything to do with attracting Jay's attention and drawing him out into the garden with her. Jay Keller had been the one making all the moves from the start. Hazily she recalled the alacrity with which he had taken up Ricky's suggestion that he take her into the garden and her heart lurched painfully. Where the hell had Ricky got to? He should be here by now to help her.

'I——' she tried again, but Jay laid a finger over her mouth to silence her.

'Not now, Helen,' he told her, his voice low and huskily seductive. 'All that will come. For now, let's take first things first.'

The finger against her mouth was removed and her

lips were free, but only for a second, because almost immediately that light pressure was replaced by another infinitely more disturbing one, as Jay's lips touched hers in a kiss so softly sensual that it made her mind spin as if the world had slipped out of focus into a gently glowing haze. As Jay's arms came round her waist a burning warmth suffused her body as if she was bathed in the heat of a powerful summer sun and not the cool, clear light of a spring moon.

'Put your arms round my neck,' Jay whispered against her lips and, too entranced to question why she did so, she obeyed him instantly, letting her fingers lace themselves in the golden silk of the hair at the nape of his neck, unconsciously pulling his head down closer to hers and increasing the pressure of her own mouth so that their lips parted simultaneously to deepen and prolong the kiss.

'Helen!' Jay's sigh was a sound of deep satisfaction, but a moment later when he repeated her name his voice had changed dramatically. 'Helen?' he said uncertainly, as his hands came up to her shoulders, not to draw her closer, but to push her slightly away from him. 'Dear God, Helen, you're having the strangest effect on me.'

Jay's voice was rough and uneven, and Helen noted with shock the slurring of several words.

'I feel . . .'

His words tailed off as he lifted one hand to his temple, the gesture jerky and unnatural, very much at odds with the smooth fluidity of movement he had shown until now, and his eyes were strangely blank and unfocused in the moonlight.

'Jay, what is it? What's wrong?' Helen cried, her voice sharp with concern. What was happening to him? He wasn't drunk: to the best of her knowledge he had had only the one whisky which Ricky had brought him, and there had been no smell of alcohol on his breath before that.

'I—don't—know——' Every word seemed an effort, as if his tongue was thick and clumsy in his mouth, and his eyelids were drooping heavily over the clouded eyes so that they were almost closed.

'Jay! Please——!'

For a moment Jay roused himself slightly, making an effort to hold his head straight.

'Can't—seem to keep my—eyes—open,' he muttered thickly then, with a faint sigh, he abandoned the effort to retain his grip on himself and subsided against her, his head resting heavily on her shoulder, every muscle limp, and his eyes firmly closed.

CHAPTER TWO

'JAY!'

For a long, fraught moment Helen simply stared, frozen into absolute stillness by the shock of what had happened. Then, very slowly and tentatively, she reached out and touched Jay's hand where it rested on the bench beside her, lifting it cautiously. It felt heavy and lifeless and when she released it it dropped back limply on to the wooden slats without any resistance, and that small thing was enough to push her into action.

'Oh my God—Jay!' She gripped his shoulders, shaking him hard. 'Jay! Wake up! Please wake up!'

But there was no response from the inert figure at her side.

'Jay—please!'

What *was* wrong with him? Once more Helen froze in horror as a new and more terrifying thought penetrated the whirling haze in her head, one that had her fumbling for Jay's wrist, her fingers closing over it desperately.

'Don't panic, Nell, he's not dead.' Ricky's voice reached her in the same second that her fingers found the reassuringly steady pounding of Jay's pulse. 'It's only the effect of the Mickey Finn I slipped him.'

'The *what*?' Helen exclaimed, swinging round swiftly as her brother and another young man came to her side, the latter taking Jay's limp wrist in his hand and checking his pulse too, nodding his satisfaction as he did so.

'We had to give him something, Sis!' Ricky pointed out. 'So we could get him out of here without any fuss. I've told everyone he's had to leave early and——' He broke off abruptly after a swift glance at his sister's white, shocked face. 'What did you think we were going to do? Hit him over the head with a hammer?'

'You've drugged him!' Helen's voice shook with disbelief. 'But is that safe? I mean—with the whisky and——'

Words failed her as she caught the look that passed between the two young men, a trifle impatient, definitely conspiratorial, and with a little too much of 'Women! Don't they fuss!' in it for her liking.

'Of course it's all right,' Ricky told her with an infuriatingly exaggerated patience. 'Jon knows what he's doing.'

'He'll just sleep very heavily for a few hours,' the other man put in, and now, belatedly, Helen remembered that her brother's friend was a medical student. 'And he'll probably have a bad head in the morning, but it won't do him any lasting harm—honest. Let's get going, Rick,' he added to her brother. 'We'd better get out of here before anyone sees us.'

Helen couldn't watch as between them they lifted Jay's inert body and half carried, half dragged him between them to the car park. She supposed that if anyone saw them they would simply believe them to be a group of young people on their way home from a party, one of their number having had decidedly too much to drink and needing assistance to stay on his feet, but she knew that the truth was very different and that made the queasy, churning sensation in the pit of her stomach ten times worse.

This wasn't at all what she had expected. She didn't know what she had thought would happen; naïvely, perhaps, she had half hoped that Jay would have been brought in on the kidnap scheme, that it could all have been arranged quite amicably with him going along on the pretence of having been abducted in order to get the publicity Ricky had been so sure he craved. But this deliberate drugging of the man, bringing him to a state of blank unconsciousness, smacked a little to much of harsh reality, not the light-hearted scheme Ricky had outlined. It was impossible not to think of terrorists and thugs and all the stories of forcible abductions she had ever heard on the news.

It was true that they intended no harm to Jay, but didn't their actions differ only in degree rather than in any true moral sense from those other more violent men? And wasn't that how Jay would see it when he finally awoke?

The thought made her shudder convulsively, reaction to the shock of Jay's sudden lapse into unconsciousness finally setting in with a vengeance, so that when Jay had been bundled into the car and it was time for them to go, she sat in the driving-seat, the keys gripped tightly in one unsteady hand, and her composure shattered once and for all.

'I can't!' she cried shakily. 'I just can't! Ricky, you'll have to drive.'

'Oh, for heaven's sake!' Ricky was already opening the rear door. 'You get in the back them—but hurry up! Someone will see us if we mess around any longer.'

Later, Helen was to remember the short drive to her home as a nightmare experience. As the car sped through the darkened streets she sat stiffly in the back seat, Jay's unconscious form slumped awkwardly beside her. At one point, as they rounded a corner, he slid slowly towards her, leaning up against her with his head resting lightly on her shoulder. Instinctively she put an arm around him to support him, cradling him close, his body a dead weight. She could feel his warmth, the softness of his hair against her cheek, she could hear his heavy, drugged breathing in the silence. The subtle fragrance of his aftershave tickled her nostrils, combining with the more potently sensual scent of his body, to set her pulse racing in a reaction that was no longer purely fear, and yet inextricably entangled with the panic that had gripped her earlier.

Once at the house, Helen gave into her feelings and fled indoors, ostensibly to make coffee, but in reality to snatch a few much needed moments of solitude to draw breath and collect her thoughts. But, try as she might, she could not close her ears to the muffled thuds and suppressed laughter that accompanied Ricky and Jon's manhandling of Jay up the stairs and into the spare bedroom. Ricky was enjoying this, she realised with a sense of shock, loving every minute of it, his wayward streak coming out into the open with the thrill of illicit action and subterfuge. Her suspicions were confirmed when her brother bounded into the kitchen, blue eyes gleaming with an unholy delight.

'He's sleeping so hard he'd not hear the last trumpet if it sounded,' he declared gleefully. 'But I've locked the bedroom door just in case. Here's the key.'

He moved forward to place the key and a sealed envelope on the table, and only then did Helen realise that neither her brother nor his friend had removed their coats. In fact, Ricky was now zipping up his padded jacket with evident determination to leave almost immediately.

'I'm making some coffee,' she said uncertainly, hoping that she had misread his actions.

'Not for us thanks, we haven't time. We've got to be off.'

'But where are you going?' Helen's voice sounded loud and sharp in the quiet house.

'We're off on the next project,' Ricky told her airily, unaware of or completely indifferent to her distress. 'We've organised a sponsored walk over part of the Pennine Way. We have to leave tonight in order to have an early start in the morning.'

'Ricky! You can't leave me like this!'

For the first time Ricky became aware of her pale, strained face and he smiled reassuringly.

'There's nothing to worry about. Keller can't wake for hours—and when he does just give him that letter. It explains everything. You can handle things, Nell,' he added with a confidence Helen was very far from feeling. 'And I'll be back at the weekend. By then I expect Jay will have paid up and gone on his way.'

'But what if he doesn't?'

'Oh, he will.' Ricky dismissed her objections lightly. 'I have it on good authority that he's due back in London on Thursday to record a new single, so he'll want to get out of here as quickly as possible. See you, Sis.'

'But Ricky——' Helen's protest was ignored and a few seconds later she was left staring at the door that had swung to behind Ricky and his friend as they made a hasty departure.

There was only one thing she could do, Helen told herself an hour later as she still sat in the silent kitchen, a long-cooled mug of coffee on the table beside her. There was only one sensible course of action left open to her and that was to take herself off to bed, to sleep away what remained of this unbelievable night, and hope that in the morning things would look somehow different—which of course they never could. In the morning Jay would still be here and in heaven alone knew what sort of a mood. He would have to be faced and the situation explained to him and—— Helen's mind was too tired to consider the possible repercussions from that confrontation.

How typical of Ricky to get her into this predicament and then swan off again without so much as a by-your-leave! That was her brother all over, full of verve and flash, but with no consistency to follow through the results of his actions. It made him a very popular member of student society, but Helen wasn't a student; she had her own life to lead, a job to go to.

Her job! Helen's head jerked up in shock. She hadn't thought about that! How could she go into work tomorrow, leaving Jay imprisoned in the spare room? Drugged or not, he would have to come round eventually. With a seething curse directed in the general direction in which her brother had departed, Helen reluctantly accepted the fact that she could not go into work the next day. She would have to ring in and say she was sick, something that went very much against the grain. She enjoyed her job, it was the one part of her life she hadn't had to rebuild after David's desertion, and she wasn't one to miss a day unless she was genuinely unwell—under normal circumstances, that was.

But these circumstances were far from normal. Damn you, Ricky! she thought furiously as, pushing herself into action, she moved to empty the cold coffee down the sink and rinse out the mug. This is the last time I get involved in any of your crack-brained schemes, no matter how praiseworthy your motives! She knew she had no alternative but to pretend she was ill. She could hardly tell her boss she had a famous rock star drugged and imprisoned in her home.

Helen took the bedroom keys upstairs with her for safe keeping—and for that reason only, she told herself firmly—but, once on the landing outside the spare bedroom door, she hesitated. She couldn't just go to bed and leave him, she had to check he was all right.

But even as she allowed herself the excuse of having a rational reason to slide the key into the lock and turn it Helen knew that she also had to admit to a secret longing to see Jay Keller once more. The memory of that kiss in the garden still lingered, a little tainted by what had happened afterwards perhaps, but nevertheless it still woke a surprisingly warm glow in her heart.

Jay was lying on his side, his golden hair tousled on the pillow and one arm hanging limply over the edge of the bed. His breathing sounded heavy and unnatural in the silence of the night, and a cold hand squeezed Helen's heart at the sound of it. Was he all right? She hoped Jon knew what he was doing. He might be in his final year, but he hadn't qualified yet. What if he had given the wrong dose, or something that didn't mix with alcohol?

That thought had her moving forward swiftly to rest an anxious hand on Jay's forehead, her nervous pulse slowing slightly at the discovery that his skin was reassuringly cool with no touch of heat or perspiration to rouse her fears. Relaxing slightly, she considered him thoughtfully, seeing him with clear eyes for the first time that night.

There was something very disturbing about what she saw. Most people's faces relaxed in sleep, their expressions softening from the tensions of daily life to a more vulnerable appearance, but this was not the case with Jay Keller. The clean-cut lines of his features looked stronger than ever, and without those wide, bright eyes to lighten his face he looked colder, more forceful.

Ricky and Jon must have undressed their unconscious captive, and now as he stirred slightly in his sleep the blankets slid down from his muscled shoulders, revealing a chest that was taut and firm and lightly covered in soft hair. He must work out with weights or something to keep himself fit, Helen thought inconsequentially, he had never got that physique from simply playing guitar on stage. Suddenly it struck her that something was wrong—or different—but she didn't know quite what. A second later she realised—the tattoo was missing; there was no sign of the tiny butterfly at the base of the strong column of his throat. So it had been only make-up all the time, as phony and calculated as the rest of his stage act.

There was something very reassuring about realising that, easing some of the sick feeling that lingered in Helen's stomach at the thought of imprisoning another human being against his will. If Jay Keller planned his act and his appearance so carefully in order to gain maximum impact, then perhaps, as Ricky had said, he would appreciate his kidnapping as a publicity stunt and might positively enjoy it.

In their haste to settle Jay and be gone, Ricky and Jon had taken very little care with his clothes, and they lay in a disordered bundle at the end of the bed in such a tumbled state that, if left, they would be creased beyond wearing in the morning. Helen moved to straighten them, her hands smoothing and folding them automatically before placing them on coat hangers inside the wardrobe—until she picked up the black shirt. The soft silk slithered between her fingers and the fragrance of Jay's aftershave and the more personal scent of his skin still lingered on the supple material so that she could almost imagine that it was still warm from the heat of his body. Her hands froze, holding the shirt close against her, her grey eyes clouding as she remembered.

'You're very beautiful, Helen.'

She could almost believe that the man in the bed had spoken, so clearly did his voice sound in her head.

'I want to get to know you—to learn everything about you.'

David had said much the same thing and she had vowed that never again would she trust the blatant flattery men indulged in without meaning a word of it, but, strangely, she hadn't spared David a passing thought at the time. It was no good telling herself that Jay Keller was a man who had hundreds of women worshipping him, fans who followed every move he made, dreamed of one word, one look from him, so that he only had to snap his fingers for them to come running; no good to know that he probably took every advantage of the situation—so many rock stars had a different woman every night, so why should he be any different? Try as she might, Helen could not suppress the warmth that spread through her body at simply remembering that kiss.

It had been one of pure physical feeling of the kind that communicated on the deepest level of instinct without need of word or explanations, and she had responded on the same level, letting her actions speak for thoughts that hadn't yet risen to the rational part of her brain.

But now they had, and Helen felt hot and then cold at the realisation of the truth about the way she was feeling. She had said, had hoped very sincerely that tomorrow morning Jay would pay up and leave—but now she had to admit that, deep down, that was the very last thing she wanted.

'I think I may have some sort of tummy bug.'

Helen was glad that Julie, Eric Frazer's secretary, could not see her as she uttered the deliberate lie. The colour in her cheeks would have given her away at once, as would the slightly too tight grip on the telephone receiver.

'I was up half the night, couldn't sleep at all.'

Well, that at least wasn't a lie. In spite of the fact that it had been well after two before she had finally got to bed, she had still lain awake for hours, kept from sleep by troubled thoughts about the man in the room just across the landing, only falling into an uneasy doze just before dawn. So now she could say with total honesty, 'I feel completely washed out. What I need is a really quiet, restful day.'

Not that she was likely to get one, she added wryly to herself as, after automatically acknowledging Julie's sympathy, she replaced the receiver. Jay would have to be faced some time and, like all unpleasant tasks, it was probably better done sooner rather than later.

But Jay was still sound asleep when, after a tentative, hesitant knock, she unlocked the bedroom door and looked into the room, her hands tightening on the mug of coffee she was carrying—as some sort of peace offering? A gesture of friendship anyway. She frowned, uncertain of what her next move should be.

'Mr Keller?'

He was lying on his back, the golden head cradled on the crisp cotton of the pillows.

'Jay?'

What *did* you call someone you had kidnapped? It seemed farcical to stick to strict formality in such intimate surroundings, and yet his first name felt uncomfortable on her tongue, so that she stumbled over it as she struggeld with a nervous desire to giggle in reaction to the tension that strung her nerves tight, a desire that faded swiftly as Jay stirred in response to the sound of her voice.

'Jay?' The name came out as an embarrassing croak. Her mind was hazy with relief at the fact that he was coming round at last, that they had done him no harm, but the relief was mixed with something close to panic at the realisation that the confrontation she had dreaded now could not be delayed a moment longer.

A sighing moan from the man in the bed jolted her into speech once more.

'Are you all right? I mean—how's your head?' Concern made her voice sharp.

Jay sighed again, lifting one hand to push it through the rich thickness of his hair, then he half raised himself on the pillows, clearly struggling to bring himself properly awake. His movement brought him directly into the path of a beam of sunlight, and for the first time Helen caught the gleam of copper among the golden strands. It really was a singularly attractive combination, she thought inconsequentially, not blond and not red, gold and copper blended together—— She started as Jay's voice brought her back down to earth with a jolt.

'OK, who the hell are you?' His eyes remained closed, and even though his tone was still slightly thickened by the drug there was no mistaking the sardonic note in it. 'The Mafia—IRA—Animal Liberation?'

This time the nervous laughter would not be held back, Helen's response as much one of a release from her anxiety about him as from any true amusement.

'None of those. We're quite harmless, really.'

'Harmless!' Jay's eyes flew open, directing the full force of that keen emerald gaze straight on to her face. 'Do you call it——' He broke off sharply, what he had been about to say dying on his lips as he focused fully at last. *'You!'*

The tone in which that one word was uttered was enough to send Helen's heart plummeting to somewhere below her sandalled feet. She wouldn't have thought it possible that a single syllable could contain such a combination of incredulity, contempt, disgust and sheer black fury as Jay injected into it, but he managed to put all that and more into his exclamation so that her own voice was shaken and uneven as she answered him.

'I'm afraid so.' No, that sounded too flippant. She didn't want him to think she took this at all lightly. For reasons about which she was none too clear she needed Jay to understand her motives for going along with this scheme—but how to begin? 'I made some coffee,' she said simply for something to say. 'And perhaps you'd like——'

'What I'd really like,' Jay cut in on her harshly, 'is to get out of this room——'

'Oh, but you can't go anywhere!' Helen protested.

'Not even to the bathroom?' The bitterly satirical tone of Jay's voice brought a wash of fiery colour to her cheeks, swamping her with confusion and embarrassment.

'All right,' she managed unevenly. 'But don't do anything stupid—don't try——' Her voice failed her as she was forced to wonder just what she would do if he did try anything. He might not be as big as Ricky, but she had seen enough of those well-honed muscles to know that she wouldn't stand an icicle's chance in hell if he did decide to react violently.

The smile that twisted Jay's lips was darkly ironical. 'As far as I'm aware, whoever put me to bed left me with precisely one item of clothing, and, much as I may want to get out of here, I'm not so desperate as to risk getting arrested for streaking down the road in broad daylight.'

The bitterness underlying the dark humour in his voice caught on Helen's raw nerves. He was hating this, she realised, hating being at such a disadvantage in front of a complete stranger—and a female at that. And who could blame him? Putting herself in his position, she would find it very hard to bear too.

'I'm sorry.' Conscience forced her to say it. 'If you wait a minute I'll get you something.'

It took only a few seconds to go to Ricky's room and collect the heavy towelling robe that hung on the back of the door, but it was as she returned to the bedroom that she realised how vital those seconds could have been. Unthinkingly she had left the door wide open. If he had wanted to, Jay could have been out of the bed and half-way down the stairs while she wasn't looking. Oh, damn you, Ricky! Once more she cursed her absent brother. If Ricky had been here she wouldn't have had to worry about such things. Really, she wasn't cut out to be a kidnapper, she added wryly, she wasn't hard enough to do the job properly.

Jay hadn't moved, he still sat in the bed, leaning back against the pillows, but it was obvious that he had noticed the mistake about the door and the wary green eyes had a frankly incredulous look in them as he watched her come back into the room.

'Do you do this sort of thing often?' he asked tauntingly as she reached his side.

'No.' Helen's voice was gruff. 'As a matter of fact it's my first time.'

'It shows,' Jay remarked with a mild satire that rocked her mental balance severely.

'Here.'

She thrust the robe at him, not meeting those vivid eyes, hating the mockery that gleamed in them and well aware of the fact that Jay had forgotten his own embarrassment in an appreciation of hers, so that the way she turned her back on him as he flung back the covers—not caring if she was wise to do so or not—was more to hide her betraying face than from any idea of avoiding seeing his near-naked body as he shrugged himself into his robe. Living with a brother as physically uninhibited as Ricky had long since destroyed any embarrassment she might have felt on that matter.

Out of the corner of her eye, she saw Jay sway unsteadily on his feet, catching hold of the bedhead for support. Immediately she swung round, a worried exclamation escaping her lips.

'Careful! You nearly fell.'

Automatically her hands went out to steady him, sliding round his narrow waist with an ease that she would have thought impossible only minutes before. Jay's arm came round her shoulders, warm and heavy, and she heard his angry curse as he lifted his other hand to his head.

'Hell, but I'm as weak as a kitten,' he muttered roughly, and Helen's heart twisted at the realisation that the fury in his voice was directed at himself and his own weakness, not at her. Not a man who liked to be less than perfect, this Jay Keller.

'What the hell did you give me?' he demanded sharply.

'I—I don't know,' Helen answered honestly. 'And *I* didn't give you anything. I didn't know about that. I——' She broke off abruptly, seeing the lift on one eyebrow that questioned the veracity of her statement, then repeated more vehemently, 'I *didn't know* about it. It was Ricky and Jon's idea to drug you.'

This time both eyebrows lifted in an expression that was very far from the taunting suggestion of disbelief of a few seconds earlier.

'And Ricky and Jon, whoever they are, just *happened* to know how to get their hands on the drugs they needed?'

Helen saw the way his mind was working and didn't like it.

'It's not what you think! Ricky and Jon aren't into drugs—they've more sense than that. Jon's a medical student at the University—he knew what he was doing. You've nothing to worry about.'

'Nothing at all,' was the dry rejoinder. 'The last thing I remember is being in a garden with a particularly beautiful woman—then I wake up here in some strange house, doped up to the eyeballs, all my clothes gone, and without one hell of an idea why I've been kidnapped—I take it I *have* been kidnapped?'

Helen's stomach clenched at the ominous hardening of Jay's tone, a sensation that was made all the worse by his use of the phrase 'a particularly beautiful woman'. She didn't want to remember that part of last night.

'Sort of,' she managed, adding hurriedly as she saw the exasperation that darkened his eyes, 'but I can explain.'

'I hope to hell you can.'

As if suddenly becoming aware of the way his arm was still around her shoulders, Jay removed it abruptly, the gesture expressive of a distaste that stabbed like the point of a sharp knife. Without that warm pressure she suddenly felt cold and lost in a most disturbing way.

'Can you stand?' she asked carefully, easing the support of her own arms to see if he was balanced. There was no repetition of the swaying that had so disturbed her earlier, so she took her hands away completely, leaving him to stand alone as he so obviously wanted. 'The bathroom's second on the left,' she added as he nodded curtly. 'I'll wait here.'

'Not going to escort me to the door?' Grim humour laced Jay's voice. 'How do you know I won't escape through the bathroom window and down a drainpipe?'

The jeering taunt snapped Helen out of her uncertain mood. She was painfully aware of the fact that she hadn't been handling things at all well; it was time she got herself and the situation under control. Jay Keller was not at all as she and Ricky had naïvely imagined. *This* man wasn't going to agree to pay the ransom unless she convinced him that she meant business. She managed a cool smile as she ticked off the points on her fingers.

'One, you couldn't get through the window, it's not big enough to let a cat in or out. Two, as you've already pointed out, you're hardly dressed for a daredevil escape down the drainpipe. And, three, unless that little performance a few minutes ago was meant to con me, you're not in any fit state to go anywhere.'

Jay's mocking expression sobered swiftly, the taunting gleam vanishing completely from his eyes. 'That was no pretence,' he growled. 'I just wish to hell it had been.'

'Then you'll come straight back here?'

A silent nod was his only response, but just as Helen was beginning to relax slightly and feel she was getting a grip on events again he ruined her composure completely by adding, 'Yes, I'll come straight back here, and when I do you're going to tell me just what the hell's going on. So you'd better have your explanation ready—and I warn you it had better be a damn good one!'

CHAPTER THREE

'OK, LADY, I've waited long enough.'

Jay was lounging on the bed, the mug of coffee Helen had made in his hand, and one leg crossed negligently over the other. He looked better, the vivid green eyes brighter, and he had made the return journey from the bathroom with no recurrence of that earlier moment of weakness. The dampness of the rich hair that fell over his forehead suggested that he had taken the opportunity to splash his face with cold water in order to drive away the last remaining effects of the sedative. He appeared relaxed and at ease, but Helen told herself privately that she would be a fool to believe any such thing. The few minutes he had been out of the room had given her time to think, to reassess the situation and become extremely uncomfortable with the results.

Both she and her brother had underestimated badly in believing that the devil-may-care image Jay presented on stage was the real Jay Keller. The man she had just encountered was a very different kettle of fish indeed. Even with his mind still clouded by drugs, he had revealed an incisive grasp of the situation and had laced his comments with a sharply ironical wit that made Helen's nerve-ends curl to think of it. He hadn't revealed his temper in shouts or even a raised voice, but it had been there in the cold gleam of those penetrating green eyes and the firm compression of his strong mouth.

He was furious at the violation of his personal freedom and his privacy, and deep in her heart Helen could only understand and sympathise with him over that; it was something that had worried her from the start and now those anxieties came flooding back in full force. It was one thing to kidnap a man who would see the situation as a joke, quite another to confine a very angry, hostile man in the intimate surroundings of her own home.

So now, 'Would you like something to eat?' she prevaricated, not at all sure how to begin. She could just hand him Ricky's letter and be done with it, but for reasons she couldn't explain even to herself she needed to do more than that. Ricky's note would probably just give a few basic facts and Helen needed Jay to understand *why* she had joined her brother in his impossible scheme.

'No food. I'm not hungry,' came the curt reply. 'And stop hedging. I told you, I want to know what all this is about—I don't know you, do I?' he added disconcertingly. 'Before last night I mean.'

'No—no, you've never met me.'

'I thought not. So I've never harmed you or your family?'

'Oh no, nothing like that.'

'Not even inadvertently?' Seeing Helen's shake of her head Jay nodded with some satisfaction. 'So that rules out revenge,' he murmured, bringing her head up sharply, her eyes widening in shock.

'Oh, please don't think that! It's nothing so serious, I can assure you.'

For a moment Jay appeared to relax as he drank some of his coffee, his watchful gaze fixed intently on her face, but a few seconds later he returned to the attack.

'Then what possible motive could you have for kidnapping me and holding me here like this?' he demanded, and she shivered as she caught the bite of anger in his voice.

'Well, you see it's——' Helen tried then faltered, her hands moving nervously over her jeans, smoothing the blue cotton over and over on her knee. Her long mane of black hair fell forward over her face as she did so, hiding her expression from Jay's probing eyes, and she was grateful for its fragile protection.

'Helen.' Jay's use of her name was hard, a warning laced with a hint of threat, and it pushed her into hasty speech.

'You remember my name?' she exclaimed in surprise.

'Of course.' Jay's tone was brusque. 'There are plenty of things about last night that are hazy to say the least, but you, lady, are not one of them. The thing I find it hard to accept is that such a lovely face could hide such a deceitful, scheming mind.'

He had done it again! Just when she had nerved herself for a full explanation, he had knocked her sideways mentally with a reminder of the way he had reacted to her the previous night—the way they had both reacted to each other, Helen corrected herself. It had been a mutual attraction, no holding back on either side. But there was no sign of that attraction now, and the memory of it would only weaken her sense of purpose if she allowed herself to dwell on it.

'This is a purely business transaction,' she snapped. 'Let's leave our personal feelings out of it.'

'Feelings?' The contempt in Jay's voice seared along Helen's rawly sensitive nerves. 'I can assure you, lady, that I have no feelings to leave out.'

Well, she had asked for that, but it didn't stop the smart that came from knowing that, whatever he might have felt the night before, it was now well and truly dead. At least she knew where she stood. The best thing she could do now was to treat this situation as the business transaction she had called it. Jay was waiting for an explanation and from the spark in his eyes he was fast running out of patience.

'I told you last night that this is the Poly's Rag Week,' she began and found to her astonishment that once she had broken the ice it was surprisingly easy to continue. 'And I said that all the proceeds from the various events were going to help the hospital's Kidney Unit's funds—do you remember that?'

A curt nod was Jay's only response.

'Well, Ricky's a student at the Poly. He's on the Rag Committee and he was asked to come up with some spectacular stunts that would bring in a lot of money. There's such a need for new equipment—portable dialysis machines that can be taken to patients in an emergency, or so that they can go away on holiday—automatic blood-pressure recorders, not to mention research and transplant operations—they're all vital if lives are to be saved. The Rag Committee had thought of all the usual events, dances, shows, the parade, a sponsored walk—but they wanted one thing that would really draw attention to what they're doing and—well——'

'Are you trying to tell me that I've been kidnapped simply as some sort of stunt?' Jay's voice was uneven with disbelief, and glancing at him swiftly Helen caught a flash of something that might have been laughter in his eyes, which encouraged her so far as to manage a hesitant smile.

'That's exactly what I'm saying. You see, we knew you were coming to the concert and we thought that if you disappeared overnight it would get into all the newspapers and——' Her voice faded as that gleam in his eyes changed into something else, something she couldn't interpret or understand, but at least it wasn't anger.

'Where's your brother now?' Jay asked, that faint unevenness still lingering in his voice. 'I'd like a word with him.'

Helen could well imagine that he might; she had one or two things she wanted to say to Ricky herself—but of course that wasn't exactly manageable.

'He's involved in the sponsored walk—it's along the Pennine Way. He won't be back today.' Not sure how to read Jay's quick frown, Helen reached into her pocket for the envelope Ricky had left on the kitchen table the night before. 'But he left you a letter. It explains everything.'

She held the letter out towards Jay, but he made no move to take it. Instead he appeared to be suddenly transfixed by the sight of his own name inscribed in Ricky's appalling scrawl across the front of the envelope. After a long silent moment he shrugged his shoulders dismissively and finally took hold of the letter.

'Just for the record,' he said as he tore open the envelope, 'it's not Jay—or Keller either, for that matter.' Then, as Helen frowned her incomprehension, he explained more fully. 'Jay Keller's just a stage name. My real name's Hyde—Cal Hyde.'

'Cal?' Helen questioned, struck by the unusual name. 'What's that short for? Calvin?'

'No, Calder—my great-grandmother's maiden name. It's become something of a family tradition to give it to the elder son.'

'The elder son?' Encouraged by this new, more approachable mood, Helen found it quite easy to ask, 'Do you have a brother, then?'

Jay—or rather, Cal as she now had to think of him— nodded. 'Just the one—Joel. As a matter of fact he was the one who dreamed up the stage name. He thought it went quite well with Hyde.' His mouth twisted wryly. 'As in Jekyll and Hyde.'

'Ouch!' Helen winced exaggeratedly at the outrageous play on words, her mind acknowledging that Ricky would have loved it in the same second that she registered the change in Cal's tone. For all his words had been light and for once almost friendly, there had been a note in his voice that, taken with his suddenly guarded expression, spoke of something held back, something he didn't want her to know. Helen was intrigued. What was it he was hiding from her?'

'Is Joel your only family?'

'Apart from my mother. My father died ten years ago.' Cal's tone was abstracted, he was reading Ricky's letter, and as Helen watched she saw his eyebrows shoot up in surprise. 'Your brother doesn't mess about, does he? Have you any idea how much he's asked for in ransom?'

'No,' Helen admitted. She had left that side of things to Ricky and the rest of the Rag Committee.

'Well, believe me, he certainly thinks big.' Cal re-read the letter, then folded it and slipped it into the envelope again. 'I'll have to think about this,' he said.

'Think about it!' Helen flinched at the high-pitched sound of her own voice. Did this mean he wasn't going to pay the ransom? What would she do then? 'Is he asking too much?' she continued more quietly.

'Too much?' Cal looked thoughtful. 'No, I suppose not—not for Jay Keller, that is—but that isn't the point.' The letter was pushed into the pocket of Ricky's robe. 'I'd want to talk to your brother before I pay up.'

'Oh, but you can't—I mean——' Helen's head reeled at the thought of having this man in her home until Ricky came back. 'He won't be back until the weekend,' she finished uneasily.

'Another three days?' Cal shrugged in the same dismissive gesture he had used before. 'I can wait.'

What had happened to that important recording date Ricky had been so confident that Jay—*Cal*—wouldn't want to miss?

'But you can't stay here!'

Clear green eyes locked with Helen's troubled grey ones, Cal's calm and deep and very cold.

'Why not?'

'Because—I can't let you stay. This is my home!'

Once more Cal's shoulders lifted expressing complete indifference to her predicament.

'You were quite prepared to have me here last night. What difference will another two days make?'

All the difference in the world. She had only agreed to let Ricky deposit Cal here because he had been so sure that the ransom would be paid the following morning.

'I don't want you to stay.' Sullen and childish as it sounded, it was all she could manage.

'That's your problem,' Cal retorted swiftly. 'You should have considered that before you started all this. What would you have done if I'd just refused to pay the ransom?' Icy green eyes searched her face mercilessly as if he was trying to probe deep into her mind and read her most secret thoughts. 'What *will* you do if I refuse? And believe me, I'm thinking of it.'

This couldn't be happening! Helen tried desperately to think of an answer, but none would come. Damn, damn, *damn* you, Ricky! You should have considered this! she thought furiously, her mood not at all helped by the quiet little inner voice which reminded her that she too should have considered this possibility.

'If I go then you get nothing,' Cal warned her.

Right now, Helen felt she was prepared to settle for that. Nothing had turned out as she had expected, least of all the supposedly easy-going, publicity-loving Jay Keller who had now turned into the aggressive and dominating Calder Hyde. She felt bruised and battered, as if the swift succession of moods that had assailed her from the moment she had entered the room had actually been physical blows.

'That's fine by me,' she muttered through lips that were stiff and tight with the effort of keeping a grip on her composure. No amount of money was worth having this creature foisted on her for a further two days, she told herself fiercely, trying unsuccessfully to suppress the pang of pained conscience at the thought of the valuable donation to the Rag funds that would be lost as a result. 'Your clothes are in the wardrobe. If you'll just get dressed and go, I'll——' She broke off in consternation as Cal shook his head firmly.

'No good,' he stated adamantly. 'I'm staying.'

'But you can't! I won't let you! I'll call the police.'

What had she said to bring that smile to his lips—a smile she didn't like, not one little bit? It was a predatory smile, almost sensual in the sheer delight of some triumph.

'Go ahead,' Cal drawled nonchalantly. 'Do just that—and when they get here I'll explain exactly how I came to be in your home. What is the sentence for kidnapping these days? Five years? Ten?'

All colour drained from Helen's cheeks, making her eyes very big and dark in her pale face. They had wanted publicity for their stunt—but not this sort!

'You don't mean that! You wouldn't!'

'I do and I would,' was the unyielding response. 'Your move, lady.'

Her move! Helen couldn't think of a thing to do, a word to say. Her mind was a complete blank. She could hardly believe he would carry out his threat of telling the police she had kidnapped him, and yet she didn't dare risk the consequences if she called his bluff. He had her in a corner and, to judge from the gleam in those cold green eyes, he was only too well aware of the fact.

'But won't someone miss you?' she managed at last, the words coming out on a shaky gasp, her fingers crossing unconsciously in the hope that for some reason that recording session had slipped his mind and her question might jolt him into remembering. But Cal's response killed that fragile hope before it had fully formed.

'I doubt it. I'd planned on taking a few days off, anyway—but even if they do that shouldn't worry you.

The more people miss me, the more publicity you'll get, and that was what you wanted, wasn't it?'

'Y-yes.'

Try as she might, Helen could not inject any conviction into her voice. She felt cold at the thought of the disruption any such publicity would bring to her quiet life. She had expected that Ricky would deal with the small flurry of good-humoured interest there might have been if the kidnapping of Jay Keller and his release the following day had gone exactly as they had planned. But if Cal stayed with her three days or more, then surely someone, his manager perhaps, would call in the police, the Press would be alerted—— A shudder shook her slim body and she turned beseeching grey eyes on Cal.

'Won't you reconsider—please?'

For a second his face altered, almost softened, but then he shook his head and the cold, hard expression was back in place, sending her spirits even lower when she saw it.

'You have very beautiful eyes, sweetheart,' Cal told her softly. 'And when you use them as you did just then, I'm sure most men would find you impossible to resist. But you forget that I have first-hand experience of just how deceptive that air of innocence can be, and I'm not taken in. I'm staying, and it would make things much easier for both of us if you would simply accept that fact.'

He paused to let his words sink in, though really there was no need. Helen could be in no doubt that he meant exactly what he had said.

'Now,' he went on. 'I believe you said my clothes were in the wardrobe. If you don't mind I'd like to get dressed.'

'Why aren't you at work today?'

The question came unexpectedly, startling Helen so that she made an awkward movement with the duster she was using in a vain attempt to impose some reality on her position by following the mundane routine of housework, knocking a vase and sending it flying. It seemed destined to crash to the floor and shatter into tiny pieces, but suddenly Cal was there, catching it in one hand and restoring it to its place on the mantelpiece.

'Steady,' he murmured soothingly. 'You'll wreck the joint if you're not careful.'

'I couldn't care less if I broke that!' Helen snapped, her voice sharpened by the tension that stretched every nerve at finding him so unexpectedly close, his nearness reminding her of the instinctive hostility she had felt when he had come downstairs, dressed once more in the black shirt and the white trousers from the suit he had worn the night before, an alien unwanted presence in her home, an intruder into her territory, so that, like some nesting bird, she wanted to turn on him and peck and scratch to drive him away. 'I've always hated it.'

The vase had been a present from her prospective mother-in-law, David's mother. It was heavy cut crystal, large and elaborate and probably very expensive, but Helen had disliked it on sight, preferring the simple lines and earthy colours of hand-made pottery. She was not quite sure why she had kept it after the relationship had broken up. She had never set eyes on Mr and Mrs Bentley since their embarrassed, discomfited departure from the church after the announcement that the wedding had been cancelled.

'In that case, I could always drop it again.' Cal's voice was light with laughter and a teasing gleam shone in the clear eyes. He lifted the vase again, holding it between one finger and a thumb, poised precariously over the tiled hearth. In spite of herself Helen found her mouth curving into an answering smile.

'No, don't. I'll give it away to some jumble sale. I don't know why I've kept it so long—it's not my sort of thing at all.'

Then, because a sudden sharpening of the keen emerald gaze told her that Cal had noticed the faint unevenness of her voice, the clouding of her soft grey eyes, and because she didn't want him enquiring into the reasons for her discomfort, she went on hurriedly, 'And in answer to your question—I'm not at work because of you. I didn't want to leave you alone upstairs, so I rang in to say I was sick.'

'Was that concern for my health or worry that I might escape without paying my ransom?' Cal enquired satirically as he replaced the vase carefully on the mantelpiece before answering his own question with a wry, 'Personally, I rather suspect it was the latter.'

'Actually it was a mixture of the two,' Helen retorted swiftly. 'I could hardly go out for the day and leave you to come round alone, not knowing where you were or what was happening.'

'Isn't that what kidnappers usually do?' Cal's soft drawl was deceptive, belying the intent scrutiny of his eyes which were fixed on Helen's face so that he couldn't have missed the way she bit her bottom lip hard in response to his murmured taunt. 'But in future I think you'd do better to go into work as usual.'

'I'll do as I please!' Did he really think she could go off to work, leaving him free to wander around her home as he liked? 'I'll go in to work or not as it suits me.'

'Do you usually take much time off?'

'Not at all.' Helen shook her head vehemently, wondering where this line of questioning was leading. Cal had changed tack very slightly and she was not at all sure what was in his thoughts. 'As a matter of fact this is the first day I haven't been to work in twelve months.'

Even after the disaster of her wedding day she hadn't taken time off, even though everyone had advised her to take a few days to recover. She had gone straight back to work on what should have been the first day of her honeymoon, seeing her job as the sanctuary she needed from the pain of her life.

'All the more reason for you to carry on as normal. Don't you think it would look rather suspicious if you suddenly started taking time off now? There must be dozens of people who saw you with me at that party,' he pointed out as Helen frowned her confusion. 'What if someone's noticed I'm missing? They could put two and two together.'

'But you said no one would—you were going to take a couple of days off.'

'And so I was,' Cal agreed impassively. 'But that doesn't mean no one's tried to contact me. My absence might raise a few questions, questions people would want answering. They'd be looking for people who'd changed their routine suddenly.'

'Stop it! You're just trying to frighten me!'

And he had succeeded, too, but she wasn't going to admit that. Ricky had hoped for lots of publicity—but for the Kidney Unit, not for Helen herself. Once more a tremor shook her slim body at the thought of the

questions that might be asked, the prospect of hordes of
reporters camped outside the house waiting for a
statement—and what if Cal carried out his threat to
accuse her of kidnapping? Her vision blurred, she took
an unwary swipe at the mantelpiece with the duster and
the crystal vase so recently replaced by Cal toppled over
and fell with a crash into the hearth, where it shattered
into hundreds of tiny fragments.

'Oh no! Helen dropped to her knees on the carpet, her
hands going out to gather up the fragile slivers of glass.
'Just look what you've made me do!' she cried
accusingly.

'I thought that was what you wanted all along.'

The laughter in Cal's voice jarred on Helen's already
raw nerves, the fact that what he had said was true doing
nothing to ease her hypersensitive state. A sudden sharp
piercing sensation in the pad of one thumb was the final
straw. She could barely see the blood that trickled from
her injured finger as hot tears stung her eyes and, in spite
of her frantic efforts to blink them back, welled up and
coursed down her cheeks. Weakly she just sat back and
let them flow.

'Helen?' she heard Cal's voice as if from a long way
away. 'Hey, sweetheart, it's only a vase.'

A rustle of movement nearby told her that Cal had
come to her side, crouching down very close to her.

'I thought you didn't like it.'

Numbly Helen shook her head, unable to speak,
abandoning any attempt to control her tears. It wasn't
the loss of the vase that had upset her, it was the
accumulation of tension and uncertainty that had been
building up from the moment she had met Cal, growing

through the long sleepless hours of the night, the fraught, unbelievable events of the morning, until, like the crystal, her composure had shattered finally and completely.

'Look, if it matters that much to you I'll buy you another.' Cal's voice was very gentle, genuine concern sounding in his tone as he reached out and took her hand, his fingers closing over it, warm and strong. Vaguely she registered the fact that his hands were harder, rougher than she would have expected from a life spent simply playing the guitar on stage.

'You can't replace it,' Helen choked. 'It was a present—from the parents of the man I was going to marry. It was the only thing I·had left. I sent all his presents back when—when——' Her voice croaked painfully and she could not continue.

'I see.' Just two words, very low, but the large hand that covered hers tightened in a silent expression of sympathy. Cal waited a careful moment before he spoke again. 'Would it help to talk about it?'

Once more Helen shook her head, almost fiercely this time.

'Talking won't change anything. It's all over and done with. We were going to be married, but at the last minute David changed his mind and the wedding was called off.' Her voice sounded stiff and tight. The story came easily enough these days, at least the bare outline, the skeleton of what had happened could be spoken, but it was the other details, the ones she had always kept back from everyone, that still hurt. 'That's all.'

'That's *all*?' Cal echoed her words on a note of disbelief. 'Helen, sweetheart——'

But Helen was not going to let that pass a second time.

'I am *not* your sweetheart!' she declared angrily, drawing herself up and away from him, only now becoming aware of how in her distress she had leaned so much towards Cal that her head had almost been resting on his chest. 'So please don't call me that!' she added, pulling her hand roughly from under his to fumble in the pockets of her jeans, hunting for a handkerchief to dry her eyes.

'Here.' Cal produced a crisp white square of cotton which he held out towards her. Mutinously Helen ignored it, deliberately continuing her search and only giving up with an exclamation of despair when it proved fruitless. It was as she raised her hand to brush at her damp cheeks that Cal moved, catching her hand in one of his and imprisoning it while he used the handkerchief to wipe the tear-stains from her face. His movements were sure and firm but very gentle, the light brush of the soft material over her skin soothing, and Helen found herself relaxing, the disturbed beat of her heart slowing and easing.

'I'm sorry,' she said tautly when Cal finally took his hand away. 'I was being rather silly. I really didn't like that vase at all. In fact, there have been many times I've longed to do just that——'

As she gestured towards the shattered vase she risked a glance at Cal's face and immediately wished she hadn't because the look in his eyes destroyed her new-found composure, jolting her heart into a wild and jerky rhythm that made her feel as if it was beating high up in her throat. Hastily she lowered her gaze to stare at the widely spread splinters of glass.

'I don't know why I went to pieces like that.' In spite of

the careful control she was exerting, the words still came out on a shaken gasp.

'Don't you?' Cal's soft question seemed to shiver over her skin, raising the tiny hairs on the back of her neck. 'Helen, look at me——' The quiet voice held a note of command that could not be resisted however much she wanted to ignore it.

Reluctantly Helen lifted her eyes to meet Cal's, seeing how dark and dilated his pupils appeared, so that his eyes were almost completely black with only a thin rim of green around the edge. Immediately it was as if she was being drawn out of herself, leaving just an empty shell behind, so that if it hadn't been for the softness of the carpet underneath her and the sharp sting of her injured thumb she could have believed that she had actually left her body and was floating in a state of suspended animation, not in the real world at all. Her one rational thought was a deep-felt acknowledgement of the fact that Cal was a devastatingly attractive male, the purely sensual impact of his physical presence affecting her as no man had done for many long, lonely months.

'Helen——' Cal began, but then broke off abruptly and, clearly forgetting everything he had been about to say, continued in a low, huskily seductive voice, 'You really have the most incredibly beautiful eyes. They're such a soft grey with just a ring of black at the edge—I've never seen anything like them. Helen——'

He didn't have to say any more, didn't have to put his thoughts into words, she could read them in his face, and already she was leaning towards him, her lips parting instinctively in preparation for his kiss, her tongue appearing briefly to moisten them in unconscious invitation, a gesture that was not lost on Cal as she saw his eyes follow the tiny movement. The few seconds before Cal's head lowered to hers seemed to last for an eternity and yet, in spite of the aching need to know the touch of that firm mouth on her own, Helen felt no desire to break the mood by making any move of her own. Like Cal, she was content to wait, knowing that the moment would come, must come, and that it would be all the sweeter for this deliberate delay.

It was the moment in the garden all over again and yet somehow subtly different, this time without the shock of the unexpected, the surprise of her reaction. This time there was a familiarity about their actions, they both knew what they wanted and there was no hesitation on either part as she moved into his arms, subsiding against the hard wall of his chest with a gentle sigh, abandoning all thought and giving herself up totally to the feelings Cal could arouse with the touch of his hard, persuasive mouth.

Her body seemed to have melted, to have become boneless, fluid against Cal's strength, her lips parting further to welcome the intimate invasion of his tongue, while her fingers slid over the supple silk that covered his arms and chest, feeling the taut firmness of muscle, the warmth of his body beneath the thin material, the insinuating scent of him pervading her nostrils. She let her hands wander where they would, smoothing, enticing, silently encouraging him to do the same, letting her caresses speak for her aching need to feel his hands on her body, her restless movements stilling only when she had her wish.

The soft cotton top she wore offered little resistance to

the determined fingers that pushed it free of the waistband of her jeans, exploring the silken flesh exposed and moving upwards slowly and irresistibly, sending shudders of delight through her in response to the slightly roughened warmth of Cal's caress.

'Helen.' Her name was a hoarse, husky sound in Cal's throat as his lips moved from her mouth, trailing soft kisses over the line of her jaw and down the delicate skin of her neck. 'Dear God—Helen!' he sighed again, lifting her from her knees as he pulled her tight against him, so that she was crushed against the muscled lines of his body, held captive in a fierce, imprisoning grasp.

But as she moved one sandalled foot brushed over the pieces of the shattered vase. The soft rustling sound the glass made impinged on the heady haze that filled her mind and brought with it the cold shock of reality.

What was she doing? How had she ended up in Cal's arms like this? No, she amended swiftly, the question was not how but why? She didn't even like this man—or did she? The answer to that wasn't easy to find. In these last few minutes the hard, domineering man she had believed Cal to be had vanished completely, to be replaced by a more gentle, sympathetic person, one she had liked very much, but she could not forget the way Cal had forced her to let him stay, the frightening threat to tell the police. That memory led her to acknowledge the appropriateness of Cal's stage name. Jekyll and Hyde—he seemed to embody both men in one person just as in Stevenson's story, where the brutal, immoral Hyde had been one and the same as the courteous, civilised Doctor Jekyll. But which one was truly Cal? Not knowing, she could not let things continue like this.

'Stop it,' she murmured softly, experimentally, as much to test her own reactions as to call a halt to the kisses that Cal still pressed against her throat, threatening to defeat her purpose completely. Then, because he evidently hadn't heard and because she wanted to prove to herself that she was in control of her actions, she repeated the words more forcefully. 'I said stop it!'

She pulled away from Cal sharply, her hands coming up to his shoulder to push him back from her when his head lifted swiftly, and the full force of those vivid green eyes locked with her distressed grey ones.

For a second time seemed to stand still. Cal didn't move, he didn't even blink, but what she saw in his face made it suddenly very difficult to breathe properly. Then at last he smiled, a slow sardonic smile that Helen hated on sight.

'Dear me,' he murmured softly. 'You do over-react, don't you? What is it? Still carrying a torch for the man who jilted you?'

'David has nothing to do with this!' And the worrying thing was that this was true. The thought of David, the fear of being hurt like that again had always held her back in her few meetings with men—she could never call them relationships—since the disaster of her wedding day. But this time she hadn't even remembered David, had thought only of Cal, of herself, and the pure, sensual pleasure she had experienced.

'It was only a kiss,' Cal pointed out, the calm reasonableness of his tone catching on Helen's nerves, twisting them so tightly that she felt they might snap under the strain. Only a kiss! It might have been just that to him but to Helen it had been a reawakening, a rediscovery of needs she had thought were buried under the scars of David's desertion.

'Yes, it was just a kiss,' she said tartly. 'But it's over now and I'll thank you not to try that again. Your kisses—or anything else—aren't welcome to me, Mr Hyde, and I want that plainly understood.'

With a brusque movement she got to her feet, her hands going automatically to adjust her clothes, her movements jerky and awkward.

'Now I'm going to get a dustpan and brush and clear up this mess.'

She was quite pleased with her voice, it sounded brisk and businesslike, carefully controlled, and she felt she could have stayed that way if Cal hadn't spoken.

'Which mess, Helen?' he questioned softly. 'The glass on the floor or the mess you're making of your life?'

CHAPTER FOUR

THIS had to have been one of the most difficult days of her life, Helen told herself as she switched off the bedroom light and sank back on her pillows, grateful for the darkness and the peace and quiet in which to think. In fact, she would rate it as second only to the ordeal of her wedding day—only then it had been everyone else who had behaved as if they were treading on eggs, thinking more than twice about every word before they spoke, never quite knowing what her reaction would be.

Her father had wanted to protect her from the fuss that was inevitable when people realised there was to be no wedding after all, had tried to insist that he would be the one who would go to the church and explain, but Helen had refused to agree. She would have to face everyone some time and it was best to do it straight away before her nerve failed her. And so she had discarded the beautiful lace gown, flinging it over a chair without a care for the fact that it might be creased beyond restoration, pulled on a sweater and jeans in an unconscious act of defiance of David's disapproval of women wearing trousers, and driven herself to the small village church where, over a seemingly endless hour, she had spoken to each and every one of the friends and relatives who had gathered for the wedding, explaining what had happened in a calm and controlled manner that hid the turmoil in her heart, only finally breaking down when it was all over and she was safely back in her parents' home.

Helen stirred restlessly on the pillows, distressed by the memories she was recalling—and yet in some strange way she found the year-old pain easier to handle than the thought of the more immediate events of the day.

Somewhere in the distance a church clock chimed and, counting the strokes automatically, Helen realised it was twelve o'clock. Midnight: the end of one day and the beginning of another. At least she was a little nearer to the weekend, to the time of Ricky's return and Cal's departure. Only another couple of days to get through, surely she could manage that?

Remembering Cal's earlier comments about her going in to work, she relaxed slightly in the darkness. If she went in to the office, she would have almost ten hours free from Cal's tormenting presence. A faint smile of relief touched her lips as she reached out and switched the alarm to 'On' and then, exhausted by the past twenty-four hours, turned her face into the pillow and slept.

'Are you sure you're ready to come back?' Julie studied Helen's face closely. 'You still look terribly pale. Wouldn't another day at home have been a good idea?'

No, it most definitely would not! Helen thought, recalling the tension that had gripped her as soon as she had woken when thoughts of Cal had come flooding into her mind. She had fled from the house like a bird winging free from its cage and she had no intention of going back until the last possible moment.

'I'm fine, honestly,' she assured the other girl. 'And I couldn't have afforded to take another day off—I'm showing a prospective buyer round the Morcar house today, remember?'

'Could I forget!' Julie raised her eyes heavenwards, shaking her blonde, curly head as she did so. 'Mr Crown was having kittens yesterday at the thought that you mightn't be in to deal with that. Do you think they'll buy the place?'

'I don't know.' Helen was flicking through the papers that were piled up on her desk. They seemed to have mounted up in her absence. Was it really only a day she had been away? It felt so much longer. 'I hope they do. That place is a real white elephant, it's been on our books for ages.'

'It'll be a feather in your cap if you can get rid of it,' Julie agreed. 'And talking of feathers makes me think of birds and a Jay in particular—so tell me about Tuesday.'

'Tuesday?' Helen frowned, puzzled, half her attention on a letter she had opened. 'What about Tuesday?'

'Oh, come off it, Helen!' Julie protested. 'You know what I mean! Tuesday night—Jay Keller.'

Helen's hands clenched on the sheet of paper she was holding. She had come to work to get away from thoughts of that man, but it seemed that even here she wouldn't escape. For one appalling moment she thought that perhaps Julie knew about the kidnapping, but the other girl's next words drove that worrying suspicion from her mind.

'You were going to the party after the concert, remember?'

A swift glance at Helen's stunned face had Julie exclaiming, 'Oh, Helen, don't tell me you were too ill to go!'

'No.' Helen shook her head slowly. 'I wasn't ill. I went to the party.'

'And did you meet him?' Breathless excitement sounded in Julie's voice. 'You lucky dog!' she said as Helen nodded again. 'I couldn't even get a ticket to the concert—they were all sold out. Well, *did* you meet him? What was he like?'

'Devastating.' The word slipped out before she had time to consider whether she meant to say it or not but, having heard her own voice say it, Helen decided she couldn't think of any description that fitted Cal half as well. He had certainly devastated her peace of mind since he had come into her life!

'Oh, I know what you mean!' Julie's wide grin was accompanied by a small, sensual shiver. 'He's got a lovely bum—and those eyes!'

She rolled her own blue eyes dramatically and in spite of herself Helen managed a laugh in response. The younger girl might have interpreted the word she had used to describe Cal in a very different way from the one she had meant, but at least they were in agreement on one point. A memory of those vividly coloured eyes floated in Helen's mind, and to her consternation she found herself thinking of other things too: the thick sweep of golden hair that angled across his forehead, the lithe, firm body, trim hips and long legs in the pale trousers. She had never actually considered the part of his anatomy Julie had mentioned, but—— Snapping out of her abstracted mood, Helen blinked hard to rid herself of the persistent and unwanted vision, casting an uneasy glance at her companion, concerned that she might have noticed her reverie. But Julie was absorbed in her own thoughts and had missed her friend's preoccupation.

'There was a big write-up in the paper—I brought it in case you hadn't seen it. You don't get a *Telegraph*, do you?' Julie was hunting in her bag as she spoke. 'Look.'

Twisting nerves made Helen's stomach lurch betrayingly as she took the folded copy of the local evening paper from Julie's hands. What if it had been discovered that Cal was missing? What if the police were already looking for him? No. That would have been the first thing Julie would have mentioned if it had happened— and one swift glance at the relevant item proved that she had no need to worry.

It was a purely factual account of the concert, topped by a large photograph of Jay Keller (for, on stage at least, that was how Helen still thought of him). She skimmed through the article briefly, her eyes going back to and lingering on the photograph , seeing the leather trousers, tight as a second skin, the silky shirt slashed deeply at the front, revealing the fake butterfly tattoo, surprisingly clear even in the grainy black and white of the newsprint. She had forgotten about this side to his character, the flamboyant showman with his audience in the palm of his hand. The photograph was Cal, and yet not Cal. The high-cheekboned face was the same, as were the mesmerising eyes, but Helen found it hard to equate the man in the picture with the one she had left in her house that morning.

'Don't worry, I'll keep well indoors,' he had teased as she pulled on her coat. 'It wouldn't do for the neighbours to see me, would it? Someone might recognise me.'

Someone might well, especially after seeing this photograph which had been so widely distributed only a day before, Helen thought grimly, unable to stop herself from wondering what Cal was doing now. Had she been a fool to trust him on his own like this? What if he carried out his threat and rang the police? She had only his word that he wouldn't do that if she let him stay until Ricky got back. They could be waiting for her when she got home— but somehow she doubted that, call it instinct, but something, some intuitive sense told her that once Cal had given his word he wouldn't break it.

Suddenly becoming aware of the way the newspaper was shaking in her too-tight grip, Helen let it drop on to the desk.

'It's a good article,' she managed. 'And an excellent photograph. It looks just like him.'

'Mmm!' Julie sighed appreciatively. 'I'm going to cut it out and keep it. Did you——?'

But Helen had had enough. She could take no more of Julie's questions.

'I think we'd better get to work,' she said abruptly. 'It's going to take me all morning to clear this lot.'

But in spite of the determination with which she sat down at her desk and set herself to dealing with the mound of paperwork before her, Helen found that her concentration was badly affected. Every time she paused to think, which was more often than she liked to admit, it was impossible to prevent her eyes going to the photograph in the newspaper which still lay on her desk, impossible not to think of the moment she had been in Cal's arms, feeling his kisses on her face and neck and— she now admitted to herself—loving every minute of it.

The smell of cooking was the first thing that greeted Helen as she let herself in through the door of her small semi that evening, a warm, savoury scent that made her mouth water immediately. She had worked through her dinner hour in an attempt to catch up on the work she had missed, and as a result she was very hungry indeed.

'Hi!' Cal greeted her casually, for all the world as if welcoming his kidnapper home from work was something he did every day, she thought on a wave of nervous laughter that she barely caught before it escaped her. 'Take off your coat and come and sit down. Would you like a drink?'

'Would I like——' Helen thought she sounded like a dazed parrot, repeating his words after him, but it was all she could manage. This was her house, and yet Cal looked so much at home that she might almost have imagined their positions had been reversed and it was *his* home to which she had returned. He looked slightly different this evening and it took her a moment or two to realise that Cal wasn't wearing the black silk shirt, but a grey and green checked one that looked vaguely familiar, Seeing her eyes on it, Cal grinned slightly.

'I helped myself to one of your brother's shirts. I couldn't wear my own for ever and I didn't bring a change of clothes with me.' Helen's cheeks burned at the satire in this tone. 'I borrowed his razor, too. I hope you don't mind.'

'No, of course not.' Helen shook her head, struggling with the feelings that pointedly ironic comment had aroused in her, reminding her quietly but firmly just why Cal was here. Being Ricky's, the shirt was very slightly too big for him, but not unattractively so, and its colour heightened the shade of his eyes, giving them a new and glowing intensity, one that held her mesmerised for a moment until Cal spoke again.

'Well, don't stand in the hall all night. You look tired. Had a busy day?'

That at least was easy to answer. 'Hectic.' With a

shrug, Helen decided to go along with Cal's way of handling things. The situation was awkward enough as it was, she might as well try and make it as reasonable as possible, she decided, as she hung her coat on a hook by the door. 'But successful,' she continued in an easier voice. 'I notched up a really good sale this afternoon— and, yes, I'd love a sherry, please.'

'Coming up.' Cal clearly knew his way round the house now, he went unerringly to the drinks cabinet, and Helen felt a spark of irritation light up inside her at his action. This was her home, damn it! With an effort she squashed her annoyance down inside her; that was not the way to put things on an easier footing. 'Sell something big, did you?' Cal asked after handing her her drink and seating himself on the settee close to her chair.

'Yes.' Helen took an appreciative sip of her sherry and leaned back in her seat, kicking off her shoes as she did so. 'A great huge ugly house that's been on the market for nearly fifteen months. The trouble was that the previous owners had done all sorts of alterations to it—they'd added a games-room, a sauna and a jacuzzi, and not many people round here could afford the price they were asking for all the extras—in fact, most of them didn't even want them! But the man who saw it today just loved it. He's going to turn the games-room into a mini gym— he's a footballer, you see.'

'Anyone I might have heard of?'

'His name was Bush—Tony Bush.'

Cal nodded knowingly. 'He's good.'

'Are you a football fan then?' Helen ventured, encouraged by Cal's quieter, more approachable mood.

'Not as much as I used to be. I played in an amateur

team when I was younger—and I was a great supporter of York City.'

'York?' Thinking of the reports she read of Jay Keller's London home, Helen was surprised. 'That's a long way from where you live, isn't it?'

Something changed in Cal's face, a sudden blanking out of expression as if curtains had just been pulled to behind his eyes.

'I was born there,' he said quietly.

The atmosphere had altered on that last exchange, becoming less relaxed, and Cal's reply was careful to the point of caginess. Perhaps after years of living in the spotlight he was reluctant to reveal much about his private life. Helen took another sip from her glass and hunted for a less emotive topic of conversation.

'What's cooking?'

'Chicken curry.' A brief grin flashed on and off. 'I hope you don't hate the stuff?'

'Oh no—I love hot, spicy food. Curry's one of my favourites.'

'Mine too,' Cal agreed. 'It'll be just about ready. When did you want to eat?'

'Soon—I'm starving. But I think I'll freshen up and change first.' She eased herself out of her chair. 'Twenty minutes OK?'

Cal's mouth curved at the corners into a slowly sensual smile.

'Anything's OK as long as you change into your jeans. You look delectable enough in that suit, but for my money those skin-tight denims you had on yesterday beat it hands down—*very* sexy,' he added in a low murmur almost to himself.

Silently Helen cursed the blood that rushed into her

cheeks. After David's stern disapproval of women in trousers, Cal's comments came as a distinct shock, as did the appreciative gleam in his eyes as he subjected her to a slow and lingering survey, his gaze sliding from her face and down over her body, that smile widening as he did so.

'I dress to please myself, Mr Hyde,' she declared sharply, embarrassment making her voice tart.

The gleam in Cal's eyes brightened, the smile becoming a broad, wicked grin.

'I'm sure you do, sweetheart,' he drawled silkily. 'I wouldn't expect anything else. I'm merely pointing out that it pleases me too—and the name's Cal, remember? I thought we agreed on that.'

'I doubt if you and I will ever agree on anything!' Helen retorted.

'Really?' Cal's tone was sceptical. 'Well, we shall have to see about that.'

'Perfect timing,' was Cal's comment when Helen returned to the living-room after rather less than the twenty minutes she had stipulated. He was standing by the record rack, flicking through a stack of LPs. 'I was just about to serve up. I thought we'd have some music while we ate.'

Make yourself at home! Helen clamped her mouth tight shut on the sarcastic comment she was tempted to make, reminding herself that, since she was responsible for Cal being here in the first place, she had only herself to blame for his intrusion into her life.

'Any preferences?' Cal lifted another record then stopped, staring at the distinctive cover underneath. 'Oh, lord,' he groaned, 'don't tell me you're a fan.'

Over his shoulder Helen saw the record he was looking

at, the carefully stylised drawing of Cal's own features with the name Jay Keller inscribed in a flowing script across the top. His latest LP, top of the LP charts for the last month.

'No, that's Ricky's. He's got every record you've ever made.'

Helen found Cal's attitude rather puzzling. She would have thought he would be pleased to discover his own work in her collection. Instead he had sounded annoyed and almost disappointed to see the record.

'Well, that's a dozen records we're definitely *not* playing. What about this?'

Helen stared in some confusion at the record he had selected.

'Mozart!' A rock singer who liked Mozart—it didn't fit, somehow.

'And why not?' Cal asked almost as if he had read her thoughts. 'You do like Mozart, don't you? I take it this is not one of Ricky's?'

'No—it's mine. Mozart's one of my favourite composers.'

'Is he?' There was a note of triumph in Cal's voice. 'I told you we'd agree on something.' Then, before Helen could recover her composure, he had swung round, the wickedly sensual grin surfacing again as he took in what she was wearing.

'I always wear my jeans in the evening,' Helen declared hastily, forestalling the comment she could see was coming. 'After having to be so smart for work I like to relax——'

'Of course,' Cal cut in smilingly as her voice faded. 'I quite understand your reasons for dressing like that—but it doesn't stop me from appreciating the way you look—

which I do—very much.' As she hunted vainly for a suitable retort he pushed the record into her hands. 'Put this on and I'll serve up the food.'

Helen would not have been human if she hadn't appreciated the meal Cal set before her. The chicken curry was exactly to her taste, the rice perfectly cooked. It was a real luxury to have someone else cook the meal, too, something she had often wished would happen on the days when she had arrived home from work tired and hungry and knowing that unless she set to and cooked there would be no food at all. Ricky was hopeless in the kitchen, making a cup of coffee was about the limit of his culinary ability, and David had always had rather rigid ideas on the subject of male and female roles. So it came as a pleasant change to find a man who was not only prepared to cook, but could do it so well that she willingly accepted the second helping Cal offered her.

'What did you do with yourself all day?' she asked when the savoury food and the wine they had drunk with the meal had helped her relax into the easier, companionable atmosphere.

'Oh, this and that—read a bit, that sort of thing. Actually, I enjoyed having the time to think.'

Think? What did he need to think about? Helen wondered. She didn't have time to pursue the question any further because at that moment Cal asked, 'Did your brother contact you?'

'No—but then I never expected he would. Swanning off like that is typical Ricky. He'll turn up when it suits him and not before.'

'He's quite a few years younger than you, isn't he?'

'Five, to be exact.' Helen nodded. 'He's just twenty— and now I suppose you're doing some mental arithmetic to work out just how old *I* am.'

'Would that matter to you so much?' Cal asked, neither confirming nor denying her suspicion. 'Why is it that women who have no need to worry are always concerned about their age? You, for example—you have the sort of bone structure that will always be beautiful, even when you're ninety.'

He had done it again! Just when she was beginning to relax, even enjoy his company, he had to come out with a comment like that, making her remember those moments in the garden, so that a feeling like prickling pins and needles set her nerves quivering, and she lowered her eyes to stare at her empty plate.

'Why do you do that, Helen? Why do you look away every time I tell you you're beautiful? Surely it's what every woman wants to hear?'

Perhaps it was, very likely it was just what most women dreamed of hearing, especially from a man as attractive and successful as Cal, but for Helen there were bitter memories attached to the words 'you're beautiful'. She could hear David's voice saying them and now, knowing just how he had meant them, the memory brought a bitter taste into her mouth.

'What is it, Helen?' Cal's voice was very soft. 'Why do I feel I've suddenly lost you? You've retreated inside yourself. What's wrong?'

'Nothing!' The sharpness of Helen's tone belied the word of denial as she pushed back her chair. 'I'll make some coffee, shall I?'

And without waiting for his answer she fled into the kitchen, closing the door firmly behind her and leaning back against it, taking slow, deep breaths to steady herself before she felt calm enough to carry out the

routine actions of making coffee. She was half afraid that
Cal would come after her, seeking an answer to his
questions, but the kitchen door remained shut, and when
she carried the two cups into the living-room she found
him sprawled in a chair, a small bundle of papers on his
knee. He glanced up briefly as she placed his cup on the
table beside him, but made no comment beyond a word
of thanks. Helen was overwhelmed by a surge of
gratitude at the way he had respected her need for
privacy, understanding intuitively that she had had to be
alone for that short time at least.

'What's that?' she asked, gesturing towards the papers
he held.

'Oh, just something I was working on today.'

Cal turned the papers, which she now recognised as
some sheets of the typing paper she used when she
brought work home, so that she could see the sketches on
them, pencil drawings of the view from the spare
bedroom window, the garden with next door's cat
perched on the fence, and the room they now sat in.

'But these are really good!' she exclaimed her delight.
'And you did them?' Cal inclined his head slightly in
acknowledgement of his work. 'What a talented person
you are—music and art——'

What had she said to put that guarded look in his eyes?
He had retreated from her—but just for a second. A
moment later he was smiling easily.

'The drawing's just a hobby. I don't get enough time to
do it properly.'

'What do you mean, properly?' Helen demanded, still
studying the pictures. 'These are as good as—oh!' She
broke off in astonishment as she saw the last sketch—a
portrait of herself as she had looked on the night of the

concert. The style of the drawing was somehow familiar and even though it was just a rough, hasty sketch, evidently drawn from memory, Cal had captured perfectly the silky fall of her long black hair, her oval face and soft, full-lipped mouth, and—most disturbing of all—he had caught the look of doubt and anxiety in her large, dark eyes. Helen's stomach cramped on a wave of reaction. She hadn't realised she had been quite so transparent.

'You weren't happy about what you were doing, were you?' Helen started as Cal's voice broke into her thoughts. She was painfully aware of the fact that he had been studying her closely as she looked at the portrait, noting the swift succession of expressions that crossed her face and clearly interpreting them correctly.

'No,' she said slowly. 'I had my doubts about the idea from the start.'

'So what made you go along with it?' Cal leaned back in his chair, his eyes never leaving her face. 'From what I've seen of you, you don't come across as the sort of person who's easily persuaded into doing something you don't want to do. Don't tell me it was just for Ricky.'

'Not for Ricky, no—but for Trish.'

'Trish?' Cal frowned his incomprehension.

'My younger sister.' Helen spoke without hesitation now, glad to get the truth out at last. 'She died of kidney failure six years ago. She was only twelve.'

'Ah.' It was a sound of satisfaction. 'Now I think I begin to understand.' Cal's jewel-like eyes had softened slightly. Helen could read sympathy in their green depths. 'No wonder you gave me such a lecture on Tuesday night. You would have been—what—nineteen—when she died? It must have affected you very badly.'

'It did.' Helen was aware of the way all colour had left her cheeks as she spoke. 'I've never felt so helpless in my life. I wanted to *do* something, anything that would help, but there was nothing I could do. I just had to watch——' she broke off abruptly, choking back a sob.

'Helen!' With a fluid, sinuous movement Cal was out of his chair and kneeling at her side, taking her hand in a warm, consoling grasp. 'Sweetheart, it's all over now. She's not suffering any more. She can't feel any more pain.'

'I know.' Helen found she didn't resent that casual 'sweetheart' any more, in fact she found it and Cal's tone very comforting, encouraging her to go on and admit to feelings she had found it hard to reveal even to Ricky before now. 'But I miss her so much, even after all this time. She was so bright and cheerful, even when she felt dreadful, and then towards the end she just seemed to fade before our eyes.'

Helen closed her eyes in pain, shaking her head to rid her mind of the pictures of Trish that filled it. She was supremely conscious of Cal's broad hand enclosing hers much as it had done the day before when he had thought she was upset about the vase, his strong sympathy communicating itself to her without need of words. Her conscience tormented her savagely at the thought of what she and Ricky had done to him and she twisted her hand in his until she was gripping his fingers tightly.

'Oh Cal, I'm so sorry!'

She couldn't say just what she was sorry for, but one swift glance at his face told her she didn't have to. His eyes had darkened until they were the sombre colour of fir-trees.

'Dear Helen,' he murmured softly. 'Does it help to know I understand? I really do understand. In fact, I'm honoured to be part of such a worthwhile scheme. I'd pay the ransom like a shot, but——'

'But what?' Helen asked unevenly when he broke off.

But Cal only shook his head. 'Not now,' he said obscurely, his tone rousing Helen's curiosity.

Why not now? she wanted to ask, but remembering his tact when she had her own thoughts that she wanted to hide, and wanting to give him the same courtesy, she swallowed down the impulsive question and said instead, 'That picture—the one you did of me—it reminds me of something.'

She reached for the sketch again, studying it more closely, then gave an exclamation of surprise as the truth dawned on her.

'The LP cover! That was your work too—a self-portrait—wasn't it?'

'I drew the picture, yes.'

Cal had got to his feet, his movement bringing a distance between them, and looking at his face Helen saw that his retreat had been mental as well as physical. There was a new tension in the muscles of his broad shoulders, and his face was set in a guarded, unsmiling expression, one that made her wonder what she had said wrong this time.

'I've always liked that cover best,' she blundered on awkwardly. 'It's so simple and yet so effective.'

'Thanks.' Cal's murmur was barely audible, his tone abstracted, his thoughts clearly on something else, until with a mental shake he seemed to bring himself back to the present.

'I'd like to do that picture properly some time. Perhaps you'd pose for me while I'm here?'

'Of course,' Helen could not iron out the unevenness from her voice. Those three brief words 'while I'm here' had brought a stabbing reminder of the position she was in. In the relaxed mood of the evening she had forgotten the other sides to Cal, the hard, calculating man who had coerced her into letting him stay by threatening to expose her to the police, and the showman, the man she could still only think of as Jay Keller, the man who deliberately flaunted his sexuality on stage, intent only on driving his fans to hysteria. She found it hard to equate that Cal with the one who had shown such sympathy and understanding earlier. Jekyll and Hyde, she thought to herself. But which was the real Cal?

The record player clicked off and Cal moved to put another LP on the turntable. It was as he straightened up from replacing the record in the rack that he knocked against something propped up against the wall in the corner of the room and it fell to the floor with a thud.

'Damn! I'm sorry—I hope I haven't damaged anything.' He bent to pick up the fallen guitar and stood upright slowly with it in his hands. 'Is this yours or Ricky's?'

'Oh, that's mine. Ricky would never have the patience to learn to play an instrument.'

'Are you any good?' It seemed an innocent enough question. Helen could see no reason for the sudden tautness of his voice.

'I had lessons at school,' she said diffidently. 'And I try to practise when I've time. I'm not up to your standard, of course,' she added, recalling his virtuoso performances in the television programme she had seen. 'And I stick to more simple tunes—folk music mainly.'

Cal nodded silently, his eyes not on her, but on the instrument in his hands. He touched the strings lightly, a thoughtful frown on his face.

'You can borrow it if you like,' Helen offered impetuously. 'If you want to practise while you're here feel free——' Her voice faded as Cal lifted his eyes to hers at last. Something had clouded their clear emerald green, making them dull and unreadable.

'No, thanks,' he said curtly.

The sharpness of his tone irritated Helen and made her voice tart as she retorted, 'Why not? Don't you think you need to practise?'

Cal's frown darkened ominously. 'It's not that at all,' he snapped. 'Thank you for the offer—but no.'

Did he have to be so brusque? Helen felt the spark of irritation flare into a flame of resentment. She treasured her guitar, it had been a twenty-first-birthday present from her parents and she rarely let anyone else touch it.

'What is it, then?' she demanded, heedless of that warning frown, not giving herself time to think if the question was wise. 'Don't you like to play just for the pleasure of it—do you only perform on stage—in front of an audience?'

The showman, she told herself, the man with an act as carefully planned and calculated as that damned false butterfly on his throat, and to her shock and consternation she realised that the feeling that shot through her was a pang of overwhelming disappointment.

'That's got nothing to do with it!' Anger flashed like lightning in Cal's eyes. 'I just don't want to borrow your guitar, surely that's plain enough for you? I don't know what the hell you're making such a fuss about.'

Don't you? Helen wanted to fling at him, but she choked the words back hastily. He would never understand them; she barely understood them herself. She only knew that in the moment Cal had refused her offer of the use of her guitar something had stabbed sharply, deep in her heart. It had hurt to have him reject her generosity, though of course he had no way of knowing how much it had meant to her, but what had hurt much more was that he had not denied her accusation of playing only to an audience.

She had *wanted* him to deny that, Helen acknowledged to herself, wanted him to prove that he was more than just the showman she had first thought him. If he had, then she would have felt better about her response to being in his arms, her delight at his kisses. She wasn't like those fans of his who worshipped blindly and thoughtlessly, she needed more from a relationship than that—or at least she had always believed she did. One of the things that had first attracted her to David had been his intelligence, his ability to talk on any subject, even those widely different from his own field of economics. The physical relationship had come later when their friendship had deepened into love—on Helen's part, at least. David had been her first, her only lover, and she had given herself to him gladly and willingly in the belief that his feelings for her had matched hers for him, only anticipating the marriage that was so soon to become a reality.

But with Cal she had found herself entering a whole new world of physical sensation and purely sensual attraction. The memory of the times she had been in his arms made her feel cold and then burningly hot as if she was in the grip of a raging fever. She hadn't thought then of intelligence or humour or any of the things of the mind she had believe she so valued; instead she had given herself up to her physical feelings as readily and eagerly as any of those screaming, hysterical fans she so despised.

Even now, when she wanted to reject such thoughts completely, her mind was refusing to obey her, registering only the forceful impact of gleaming golden hair laced with those glints of copper, jewel-bright eyes, and a strong lithe body, every inch of it taut and firm, not an ounce of excess weight to blur its outline in the slim-fitting trousers and shirt.

Mentally she gave herself a reproving shake, determined to rid her mind of such tormenting thoughts, but in vain. She was hypnotised by Cal, drawn to him like a moth to a candle flame, and she knew that if she didn't take very great care then, like that moth, she would be drawn in completely and shrivelled into ashes in the heat of a desire that left no room for any other more rational consideration.

CHAPTER FIVE

'HOME time at last!' Julie stretched luxuriously and reached for the cover to her typewriter with a sigh of relief. 'I'm dying to get out of here, aren't you?'

'I—well, yes, I am.' Helen's reply surprised even herself. Under the circumstances, it would have been quite understandable if she had viewed the end of the working day and the prospect of another evening spent in Cal's ambiguous company with something approaching dread, but in fact her reaction was quite the opposite. To her complete consternation she had found that her work did not absorb her as it usually did, time had dragged painfully slowly, and from four o'clock onwards she had been itching to put down her pen, snatch up her bag and head for the door.

She hadn't seen Cal at all that morning. He had stayed in his room during the undignified rush that had been the result of her sleeping through the alarm, leaving her barely half an hour in which to wash, dress and get to work on time; and, as she had gone to bed early the night before, pleading a tiredness that was no lie after her two disturbed nights, it was almost twenty-four hours since she had spoken to him.

'Doing anything special tonight?' Julie was pulling on her jacket.

'No—I—I don't know.'

The younger girl's face filled with undisguised curiosity at Helen's uncharacteristic hesitation.

'What is it?' she asked. 'Some man—you're not sure if he'll come round or what?'

Helen's automatic move to shake her head was stilled suddenly as she had second and then third thoughts about her denial. She wouldn't be waiting in for Cal, she knew only too well he would be there. It was only Thursday, there was still a day and half before Ricky would be back—but in a way Julie's words were true. It *was* a man who had her hurrying home like this. The truth came as a shock, but she faced it squarely and honestly. The day had been so long because she was *missing* Cal. After only forty-eight hours she was addicted to the sight and the sound of him, he was like a drug to her and, like a true addict, she was already suffering withdrawal symptoms after only a few hours without him.

'Something like that,' she managed in answer to Julie's query and saw the other girl's face break into a wide grin.

'Lucky you! All I've got ahead of me is a date with the ironing-board.' She picked up her bag and slung it over one shoulder. 'Now what I'd really like is to get home and find Jay Keller waiting for me with a meal already cooked and a long, long night before us. Some hope!' she turned towards the door, completely missing the swift rush of colour to Helen's cheeks. 'Still, I can always dream. 'Night!'

Cal *had* cooked a meal for her again, and Helen could not suppress the smile that curved her lips as soon as she smelt the savoury aroma of the food. This was Julie's dream exactly, the man, the meal and—her smile wavered as Julie's final words rang in her head. And the long, long night ahead of us? she asked herself and found that the answer came surprisingly easily. Yes, that was what she wanted, too.

Helen's smile resurfaced with a slightly more determined air as she took off her coat. Her fears of the previous night were forgotten as she admitted to herself that this *was* what she wanted. She wanted to get to know Cal, learn more about him—and tonight was the perfect opportunity.

Her steps were light as she went upstairs to change, zipping herself into her jeans without a qualm, well aware that she had chosen to dress this way quite deliberately. Cal had said how much he liked her in such clothes and the thought brought a warm glow to her cheeks, a sparkle to her usually cool grey eyes as she surveyed her reflection in the mirror. She wanted to please Cal, wanted him to find her attractive—hopefully as attractive as she found him—and they would take it from there. And when a memory of David surfaced in her mind she pushed it away determinedly, refusing to think about her ex-fiancé. This time was different. Ricky had been right, she had been hiding away too long, denying her most feminine needs in her determination never to be hurt again. Tonight was going to change all that.

'One thing's been puzzling me,' she said later, towards the end of the meal which they had shared in a companionable mood of easy, trivial chat. Cal lifted his head and directed an enquiring glance in her direction.

'And what's that?' he asked.

'On Tuesday, when we met——' She could picture it clearly, recalling as vividly as if it was actually happening now, the impact of those clear green eyes, the coolly cynical voice saying, "So did you enjoy the all-singing, all-dancing, never-standing-still Jay Keller spectacular?".

'When you talked about the concert, you sounded as if you hadn't enjoyed it.'

'You could be right.' Cal's voice was giving nothing away, his tone as non-committal as his expression, but Helen didn't have his ability to conceal her feelings and she knew her surprise must show on her face.

'And the party?' she questioned and saw Cal's shoulders lift in a dismissive shrug. 'That wasn't your sort of thing either?'

'Lord, no! I hate crowds.'

For a second Helen was speechless. Cal's reaction was so totally unexpected. What had happened to the showman who enticed and seduced his audience so deliberately?

'You—? That must make things very difficult for you,' she said, thinking of the hundreds of people who had flocked to the hall on Tuesday night. Not being keen on crowded places herself, she had found even the party difficult enough to cope with. 'How do you manage?'

Cal's smile was slow and warm. 'I usually find some beautiful girl and entice her into the garden with me,' he murmured silkily.

It was impossible to control the wash of pink that coloured her cheeks, impossible to conceal the sudden racing of her pulse that quickened her breathing and was betrayed in the rapid rise and fall of her loose blue and white striped shirt. 'Some beautiful girl'. 'Some *beautiful* girl'. The words echoed over and over in her head. Her mouth and throat felt dry and she had to swallow hard to relieve them, her delight in that 'beautiful' mixed with a bitterness that came from the implications behind what Cal had said. How many other girls had there been? How many moonlit nights weaving a magic spell that combined with the sheer sexuality of his physical presence to draw each and every one of them into his arms?

'Like me?' she managed awkwardly, hiding the savage stab of pain behind a stiffness of tone.

Cal's smile grew wider. 'Oh no, Helen,' he told her softly. 'None of them were at all like you.'

Then, clearly anticipating her instinctive desire to lower her head, to look anywhere but into those searching green eyes, he suddenly leaned forward and put his hand under her chin, lifting her head so that unless she closed her eyes she was forced to look straight into his face.

'Don't do it again, Helen,' he said huskily, almost pleadingly. 'Don't retreat—don't hide from me.'

Hiding! That was what Ricky had accused her of doing, what she had realised was just what she *had* been doing—and because she had wanted tonight to be so very different Helen fought her impulse to pull away from that gently restraining hand and let her wide, soft grey eyes meet the full mesmeric force of his green ones head on.

'I'm not hiding from you, Cal,' she assured him, her voice low but firm. 'It's just that there must have been hundreds of girls.'

'Hundreds!' Cal's chuckle was a warm sound in his throat. 'Dear God, Helen, what do you think I am—Casanova himself?' Abruptly his expression sobered. 'Helen, do you remember what I told you on the night we met?'

'You—I——' Helen's tongue would not form the words. It seemed as if the touch of Cal's hand on her face, the hypnotic force of his eyes had drawn all the strength from her mind so that she was unable to speak or even to think of an answer.

'I told you that you were the most beautiful woman I had ever seen, and I meant it. I still mean it. It wasn't the moonlight, it wasn't the drugs affecting my brain, it wasn't just some line I was giving you. You are, quite simply, the most devastatingly lovely creature I have ever met. I've never seen anyone who even comes close.'

If only he knew the importance of those words to Helen. If she could only believe them, they would mean more than anything else that had gone before.

'Surely you must have met someone who looks a little like me.' He had travelled so much, met so many people. In all his years in the spotlight he must have seen thousands of other women.

Cal shook his head firmly. 'No one,' he declared adamantly.

'Oh, but you must have!' It came out on a nervous laugh, the strain of trying to suppress unwanted memories showing through in her voice. 'They say everyone has a double somewhere in the world.'

She had meant it to sound like a joke, but the sudden catch in her voice betrayed the fact that it was more than that, and the effect of her words on Cal was dramatic. The smile faded swiftly from his face and the hand that still held her chin dropped to the table, then moved to his glass, to his knife, to straighten them quite unnecessarily.

'So they do,' he said flatly. 'Helen——'

But Helen was lost in private thoughts and memories, memories of David and a story as old as the hills. It was an age-old tale of love found and lost, it had happened many times before and it would happen again, but that did not make it any easier.

'I'm—very flattered,' she blurted out hastily, wanting

to blot out the pictures that were forming in her mind. 'But——'

'*Flattered!*' Cal's voice was harsh. 'Damn you, Helen, I wasn't flattering you! I meant every word I said.'

He pushed his chair back with a violent movement and stood up, swinging away from her and thrusting his hands deep into the pockets of his trousers, his shoulders hunched against some strain that she could sense intuitively, but could not even begin to guess the reasons for. Helen bit her lip hard. She had wanted to get to know Cal, but it seemed she had driven him away from her and she didn't quite know how. Slowly she got to her feet, moving to Cal's side and tentatively reaching out a hand to rest it on his arm.

'Cal, I'm sorry. I didn't mean it like that. Can't we start again?'

For a moment she thought he was about to refuse, shake off her hand with an angry movement, but then he turned slowly, giving her a rather rueful smile.

'I think that would be a good idea,' he said quietly. 'We didn't exactly start out on the right foot from the very beginning, did we?'

His lop-sided, rather shamefaced grin made him look boyish and strangely vulnerable, making Helen want to reach out, draw him close to her. But the time wasn't right for that yet, so instead, hunting for something to bridge the gap between them, Helen thought she had found the perfect answer.

'You said you wanted to draw me properly,' she suggested diffidently. 'Would tonight be a good time?'

'Tonight would be the perfect time,' Cal assured her. 'And we can talk while I work.'

For the next hour or so it seemed to Helen as if Cal's

sudden outburst had opened the floodgates, washing away the barriers of restraint between them, so that suddenly they were talking like old friends, filling in the details of their lives before they had met, Helen opening up about Trish and her brief, sad life, though she avoided all mention of David and the pain he had caused her, and Cal offering in return an account of his boyhood in Yorkshire and the farm his father had owned on which he and his brother had grown up. Helen was frankly surprised at the enthusiasm he revealed for the country-side and the outdoor life; it was all a far cry from the sophisticated, tinsel world of show business, and rock music in particular. How would she have felt, she wondered, if Cal had not been Jay Keller, if that farm and the way of life it offered had been his instead of the showmanship of the career he had actually followed? She could have been very happy with that, she told herself with a pang of regret for what could not be and for the fact that her distrust and dislike of his showbusiness personality must always come between them.

In between the talk there were times of silence, times in which Cal's pencil moved swiftly and surely over the paper, pausing only when he cast a swift, searching glance at her face before turning his attention back to his sketch to capture what he saw on the paper. Helen welcomed these silent moments when he was absorbed, because then she could let her gaze rest on the bright sheen of his hair, the strong, clean angles of his face, the sure, confident movements of his hands.

A glowing, sensual warmth filled her veins with a memory of how it had felt to have those hands touch her skin.

'What are you grinning about?' Cal asked idly,

catching a smile she hadn't even been aware of as he glanced up. 'You look like the cat who got the cream.'

'I was just thinking that I like having you here,' she told him, coming as close to the truth as she dared.

That shook Cal slightly. The green eyes he turned on her face were frankly surprised.

'I like being here, too,' he said slowly, after a moment's pause. 'There—that's finished.'

He added one last touch of shading to the picture and turned it so that Helen could seen the finished result.

'Your portrait, madam.'

'Oh, Cal, it's lovely!' Helen exclaimed her delight. For all the features of the girl in the picture were so very familiar to her, she could hardly believe the portrait was of herself. Seen through his eyes, she was, after all, surprisingly beautiful. 'It's very——'

'Flattering?' Cal supplied the word drily. 'I simply draw what I see, Helen, and what I see is an exceptionally lovely woman.' The emerald eyes had a distinctly challenging light in them now, but Helen was ready for him, and she met his penetrating gaze with an open smile.

'Thank you,' she murmured softly and was startled by his laugh of triumph.

'Success at last!' he declared delightedly. 'I do believe we're getting somewhere. Tell me,' he went on more seriously, dropping the portrait on to the coffee-table and leaning forward, 'why do you find it so damned hard to accept a compliment?'

But that was a question Helen wasn't yet ready to answer, and so with a careful pretence at misreading Cal's words she turned her answer into a joke.

'If you had a brother like Ricky you wouldn't be too used to compliments either.' She managed an uneven laugh. 'I think his kindest name for me when we were young was Fishface.'

'Charming!' Cal's tone was light, but his eyes told her that he wasn't going to be dissuaded so easily, and that realisation had her searching for something, anything, that would direct their conversation off down another path, one leading well away from any subject that might come close to her memories of David.

'You said you had a brother too. What does he do?'

'Joel?' It came out flatly, almost reluctantly, and for a moment Cal's eyelids hooded his eyes, hiding their expression from her. There was something wrong here, every instinct told her that he was unwilling to talk about his brother—but why? Had there been some quarrel?

But Helen's questions were never answered, for at that moment the telephone shrilled loudly in the hall and she got up reluctantly to go and answer it.

'Speak of the devil,' she said, coming back in to the room a short time later. 'That was Ricky! He'd finally decided it was time he got in touch with me. He wanted to know how things had gone on Wednesday.'

'And what did you tell him?'

That was a difficult question to answer. Just what would Cal's reaction be if she admitted that she had told Ricky everything had gone as planned, implying if not actually stating that Cal had paid up and departed on the day after the kidnapping?

'I—said everything was under control.'

One blond eyebrow flicked upwards sharply as if expressing doubt as to her statement, but Cal made no comment, simply asking, 'Did he say when he'd be back?'

'Yes—Saturday, some time in the afternoon.'

'Good.' Cal stretched lazily, drawing the borrowed shirt tight across his chest, emphasising the firm lines of taut muscles. 'That means I'll be out of your hair by Saturday evening. I have to admit I'll be glad to be able to go outside, too. Being indoors like this all the time is beginning to get to me.'

'Well, you could always——' Helen began but, clearly anticipating what she had been about to say, Cal broke in on her.

'Yes, I know I could pay and go—but I'm not going to. I told you, I want a few words with that brother of yours and it looks as if the only way I'm going to get them is by staying here, so that's what I'm going to do.' He stretched again, sighing deeply as he eased muscles cramped by being still too long. 'Lord knows, though, I'll be glad when I can get out and about again.'

His words stung sharply. Was he so keen to be gone, to leave her? She had only just admitted to herself how much she enjoyed having Cal here like this, how much his presence in her home had come to mean to her, but it seemed he felt nothing like that. How was she going to feel when he did finally leave on Saturday?

Helen's heart twisted painfully at the recollection of her telephone conversation with Ricky. She hadn't been able to explain the impulse that had led her to pretend that Cal had paid his ransom and gone, but if she was honest she now knew why she had done it. If she had so much as hinted at the fact that Cal was still here, if she had mentioned his threat to tell the police, then, knowing how she had felt about having him in her house in the first place, Ricky would have abandoned his sponsored walk and caught the next train home, she was sure of that—and that was precisely what she did not want. She wanted a little more time alone with Cal, time to probe under the surface of his undeniable appeal, and find out if there was anything deeper underneath.

'What you need is some fresh air and exercise,' she said a little tartly, hiding the smarting disappointment of Cal's words under a pretence of sharpness.

'What I need——' Cal echoed her, his slow smile distinctly sensual. 'Oh, Helen, *that's* not what I need.'

There was a faintly challenging light in those distinctive eyes now, one that Helen wasn't sure she was ready to meet. She was drawn to this man like a needle to a magnet, intoxicated by the potent force of his glorious masculinity. Sitting opposite him like this, it was impossible not to let her eyes dwell on the firm, lithe body, the broad shoulders and tapering waist and hips, the glorious mane of his hair. Just looking, she felt her pulse begin to quicken in response to the pull of his attraction—but whether she was prepared to take things any further was a different matter, one she hadn't yet decided in her own mind.

'Helen,' Cal muttered hoarsely. 'Dear God, Helen!'

'Cal.' Helen's whispered response was low, only a thin thread of sound, but Cal heard it, catching the note of acquiescence in the single syllable, and with a deep sound low in his throat he reached for her and captured her lips.

And now there was no time for words or thoughts, only for reaction and sensation, the vibrant awareness of total concentration on another person that drove away all doubts, all other feeling from her mind as she abandoned herself to Cal's embrace, drowning in sensual awareness, overwhelmed by burning desire and the aching longing to communicate that feeling to the man who held her. She had no chance to consider her motives, could not have brought any degree of coherency to bear on the subject, she was driven by pure blind need, wanting only to know that Cal felt that need too. She wanted to reach out and gather him close to her, hold him and keep the moment for ever, and the intensity of her longing overwhelmed her, making the ground insubstantial beneath her feet.

As she pressed her slender body close up against the firm lines of Cal's she felt the shudder that ran through him and knew that he too felt the electric current of emotion that had possessed her, so that her mouth curved into a smile of pure delight beneath his. It didn't matter that they were almost complete strangers, it no longer mattered that Cal had forced himself on to her, blackmailing her into letting him stay with threats of telling the police, or that she had so distrusted that showmanlike personality he had revealed on stage, all that mattered was what was happening here and now, when they both felt the need and the longing and shared them unrestrainedly. They were a man and a woman caught up in the most primitive, most wonderful of all sensations. It was what she wanted, what every instinct was urging her to take. It was a mutual experience and it was *right*.

'Helen!' Cal's voice was rough and uneven, his green eyes hazy with the passion that burned in her veins so that she smiled her joy straight into their depths, glorying in the effect her smile had on him as she saw him catch his breath sharply. 'Helen——' he tried again but she laid a gentle finger on his lips to silence him as, taking him by the hand, she drew him towards the settee, pulling him down beside her.

She curled her legs up on to the cushions, never releasing Cal's hand so that he had no alternative but to stretch himself out beside her, his body pressed against hers at breast and hip and knee. Helen's grey eyes never left his green ones for a second, silently speaking the message that seemed etched into her brain, willing him to know that she felt no doubt or fear, that this was what she wanted and what she prayed he wanted too.

'Kiss me,' she murmured softly, enticingly, and sighed in contentment as he obeyed her and she felt the pressure of his mouth on hers, hesitant and strangely tentative at first, then increasing its force as she opened her lips willingly to him, letting him deepen the kiss as she arched against him, her body speaking for itself, offering itself to his caressing hands.

It was Helen herself who guided Cal's hands to the buttons on her blouse, forcing herself to lie passive as he slipped each one from its fastening, but at the touch of his fingers on her aching flesh her control broke and a second later she was tugging at his shirt, fumbling with impatience, relaxing only when she felt the smooth warmth of his skin, the soft crispness of hair on his chest beneath her questing fingertips.

'Cal! Oh, Cal!'

His name was an incoherent murmur of joy, breaking off on a gasping sigh as his mouth followed the path of his hands down from her throat and over the soft swell of her breasts and into the valley between them. When his lips closed over one nipple, tugging softly, she moaned aloud, writhing beneath the hard weight of his body, her mind spinning in a mindless ecstasy of glorious yearning. Overwhelmed by the burning longing that suffused every nerve, she was greedy for more, impatient to bring events to their natural conclusion, her fingers digging into the muscles of Cal's shoulders and back as they moved lower, sliding down to the narrow waist.

But suddenly Cal's hands closed over her wandering fingers, stilling their movement. A swathe of bright hair had fallen forward into his eyes and he tossed it back with a restless movement as he turned a searching, burning look on her flushed face, holding her frozen with the mesmeric force of his vivid eyes.

'Helen,' he said gruffly. 'Helen, we have to talk.'

Talk. The word sounded harsh, alien to the mood that possessed her. She didn't want to talk, she wanted Cal to continue to make love to her, wanted to give herself to him, wanted to know the moment of his full possession. With a small, mock-sullen pout she pulled her hands out from under his, disturbed by the sudden tension in his face, the strange look that clouded his eyes, seeming to distance him from her. She wanted desperately to break down that distance and bring him closer to her again.

A faint smile touched her lips as instinct told her how best to distract him from his purpose. With a soft, sensuous movement she slid her freed hands up around his neck, tangling in the silky softness of his hair as she pulled his head down to hers.

'No words,' she whispered against his mouth. 'No words, Cal, let's just let our hands and lips——' She pressed hers on his half-yielding mouth as she wriggled even closer '—and our bodies do the talking.'

With a groan of surrender Cal abandoned all attempt to say anything further as he gathered her up, lifting her bodily from the settee, and carried her upstairs to his room where he laid her gently on the bed, his body just a dark shadow above her in the gathering dusk.

Helen had no time to think as he undressed her carefully with many caresses and soft, tormentingly tantalising kisses, but when he stood back to remove his own clothes a faint chill struck her body. Even for those few, tiny seconds she missed his closeness so terribly that when he came close again she reached for him blindly, her arms coming round him urgently, drawing him down to her with a strength she hadn't known she possessed, and from the moment that his body covered hers, warm and hard and faintly gleaming in the moonlight, she had no room in her mind for thoughts of anyone or anything else. There was only herself and Cal and the blazing, soul-shattering passion that raged between them.

Their kisses grew more demanding, their caresses less gentle, each of them rousing the other to the peak of desire and yet not moving to the final act of possession, prolonging the seconds of desire into the sweet anguish of need until in one blinding, searing moment they were no longer two separate people but one, fused in a unity of giving that suspended time and held them enclosed in a golden, glowing private world.

CHAPTER SIX

HELEN was the first to wake in the morning, stretching languorously in the warm cocoon of bedclothes and smiling sensuously as her hand touched the warm, hard strength that was Cal's body, as naked as her own. Still keeping her eyes closed, she ran her fingers slowly down the smooth length of his back, her smile widening as she felt him stir under her touch and heard his soft murmur deep in his throat.

'Good morning,' she whispered in his ear, her breath stirring his hair as she spoke.

With a great sigh Cal turned on his back, sliding an arm around her waist and drawing her close up against him before subsiding back into sleep. Helen laid her head on his shoulder and let her eyes open slowly and lazily, gazing up at the cream-painted ceiling with a dreamy contentment. Her body felt heavy and totally relaxed, Cal's warmth enclosed her and the musky scent of his body filled her nostrils so that for a while she was content simply to lie there, revelling in the slow, sensual awakening in contrast to the usual strident sound of the alarm bell jolting her from her sleep and into her brisk, efficient routine of getting dressed and ready for work.

Helen turned her head slightly to look at the face of the man sleeping next to her. As her eyes rested on his beautifully shaped mouth her own lips curved at the memory of his kisses, demanding and passionate, in the darkness of the night. The longing to rouse him, to feel the pressure of his mouth on hers once more was almost irresistible, but even as she considered doing just that some inner biological clock warned her that time was passing and, reluctantly, she pushed the thought aside. Twisting in the circle of Cal's arms she put her mouth close to his ear again.

'I hate to tell you this, but I'm going to have to move.'

Cal's response was a murmured sound of denial as his arms tightened round her. Helen laughed softly.

'Cal!' Her tone was lightly reproving. 'I have to get up. I'm a working girl, remember? I'm due at the office at nine—I have to go.'

'No.' Cal still hadn't opened his eyes and his voice was slurred with sleep. 'Stay here—with me.'

If only he knew how tempted she was to do just that. The bed seemed a warm, safe haven, the world outside cold and uninviting in spite of the crisp sunlight that filtered through the curtains. But she had already taken one day off this week.

'I can't, Cal. I've a job to do. Mr Crown——'

'Mr Crown can go to hell,' was the muttered reply as Cal drew her hard up against him, his lips seeking her cheek. Helen forced herself not to respond to his enticing closeness.

'I can't stay, Cal, and you know it! I need my job. We can't all be millionaire rock stars who can take a day off whenever they want to.'

That brought Cal suddenly wide awake, the vivid green eyes snapping open to stare straight into hers, an unfathomable expression burning in their depths.

'Helen——' he began, and his voice had changed, the thickness of sleep gone completely, leaving it crisp and decisive.

But in the moment that he had woken properly Cal's

grip on her waist had slackened and Helen was determined to take full advantage of the moment of freedom. With a small wriggling movement she eased herself free from his loosened hold and swung her feet out of the bed.

'Not now,' she said firmly. 'I'm late as it is. Anything else will have to wait until tonight.'

That didn't please him. The muscles of his face tightened, the emerald eyes growing cold and distant as if a shutter had suddenly banged shut behind them. Helen's light mood vanished at the sight, but then revived again at the thought that this man, whom she had so desired and who had taken her beyond the boundaries of sensual experience to a delight she had never fully experienced before, was so reluctant to let her go, even for a few hours. Her heart sang, her lips curved into a wide smile and she was tempted to forget her responsibilities and get back into bed with him. But then the distant chiming of a church clock brought her back to reality.

'It's only for a short time, Cal,' she told him, lightening her refusal with a gentle kiss brushed across his forehead before she dodged back, neatly avoiding his arms, which reached out to pull her down to him again. 'Surely you can wait a few hours,' she teased lightly.

'It looks as if I'm going to have to.' Cal's tone was resigned. 'All right, tonight then——'

'Tonight,' Helen promised softly. 'After all, it's Saturday tomorrow—we'll have all the morning then. Ricky won't be back until the afternoon.'

Now what had she said to put that troubled look back in his eyes? Could it be that, like her, Cal viewed Ricky's impending return with reluctance, seeing it as the end of this isolated idyll of time together? The thought was enough to send her hurrying through the process of washing and dressing with a soaring heart, even the most routine of actions having a whole new meaning because Cal was in her life.

This glorious mood of heightened sensitivity stayed with her all day, carrying her through her work with a new ease, spreading a golden glow over everything she did. Every task seemed easier, every colour brighter, and even her irascible and unpredictable boss was in one of his better and more approachable moods.

'It seems the wonder-man did turn up after all,' Julie commented at coffee time, after a morning during which Helen had hummed incessantly under her breath as she worked, unable to suppress the ridiculously wide grin that stretched over her face every time her thoughts wandered to Cal—which was about every second minute. 'I take it you had a good time last night?'

'Wonderful!' Helen assured her, a lilting note of joy in her voice. 'And I'm seeing him again tonight.'

'Lucky you.' Julie's face lit with an answering smile in response to Helen's enthusiasm. 'I'm really pleased for you—and a little surprised.'

'Surprised?' Helen turned a puzzled frown on the other girl. 'Why's that?'

'Well——' Julie looked embarrassed. 'I hope you don't mind me saying this, but in the time I've known you there hasn't exactly been a string of men in your wake. I rather got the impression that you weren't interested.'

'No.' Her expression sobered. When Julie had joined the firm nine months before, Helen had been in the throes of the dark despair that had gripped her since David had jilted her, wandering round in a dark fog, lost and alone. 'It was a bit like that,' she admitted.

'A bad experience?' Julie hazarded. 'Got burned, did you?'

Helen nodded. 'Badly burned. For a long time I thought I'd never trust a man again.,'

'But this new man's changed all that, hasn't he? He's obviously very special, your feet haven't touched the ground all morning. It must be love.'

Love. The word reverberated in Helen's mind, rocking her sense of reality, every instinct screaming at her to reject what Julie had said. Trust and love were two words that had been so much a part of her relationship with David, but she had never even stopped to consider them where Cal was concerned. For a long, stunned moment she stared down at her desk, recalling the events of the previous night and trying to recognise herself in the person she had been then.

With David she had held back at first, waiting, letting things develop until she had been sure enough of her feelings—and David's—to commit herself to a physical relationship, but with Cal there had been no thought of delay. In fact—her cheeks coloured faintly at the memory—she had been the one to take the initiative when Cal had hesitated so unexpectedly. She had had no thought then of love or trust, only of the soaring delight and the joy of knowing that she was wanted by this man whom she wanted so much. She doubted if she could ever feel anything close to love again. David had hurt her so terribly that her capacity to feel any such emotion had died on the morning of her wedding day. She had loved and trusted him, and all that love had brought her was pain and disillusionment.

But Cal had touched *something* in her; just to think of him made her feel alive and awake in a new and very exciting way. She was living again after twelve months in an emotional limbo, and for now that was enough. When Julie's belief that her behaviour was that of a woman in love insinuated itself into her mind again she pushed it away ruthlessly. Never again did she want to expose herself to such a loss of control; that way she was too vulnerable, too open to the sort of hurt David had inflicted on her, With a determined movement she put down her coffee-cup.

'Back to work,' she said firmly. Work would while away the hours, fill the time until she could be with Cal again.

The atmosphere hit her as soon as she opened the door to her home that evening. It was impossible to say what had changed, for the life of her she couldn't guess what it was that made her pause in the doorway, her key still in her hand, the hairs on the back of her neck lifting in an instinctive, prickling recognition of trouble, like those of a wary animal scenting a trap.

On the surface nothing had changed; everything was just as it had been on the two previous nights with the table set for two, the scent of food on the air, and the faint sounds of Cal's movements in the kitchen—and yet something was very different. Slowly she removed her coat and moved into the living-room, frowning her uncertainty.

'Welcome home.'

Cal had appeared in the kitchen doorway and one look at his face told Helen that here was the source of her unease. The warm, open expression of early that morning had gone, concealed behind a controlled rigidity that sent her heart plummeting like a stone to the ground. What had happened in the few short hours she had been away from him?

Throughout her journey from town she had been thinking of this moment, dreaming of her homecoming, imagining that she might just have time to get through the door before Cal caught her up in his arms. She had believed that they would take up exactly where they had left off, but now she was forced to admit that such imaginings had been blind delusions. It seemed that the Cal she had dreamed of no longer existed; it was as if the previous night had never been.

Or did she have it all wrong? Was Cal perhaps not too sure how to treat her? After all, it had been an abrupt and dramatic change from their tentative beginning to get to know each other to the blazing passion that had burned them up the night before. With a careful effort Helen wiped the doubt from her face and made herself smile.

'Hi!' Her voice sounded as easy and unconstrained as she could have wished. 'Had a good day?'

On an impulse she moved forward to press a swift, light kiss on Cal's cheek and immediately all her doubts returned with a vengeance. She could feel the tension in the muscles of his face, held taut and rigid with the effort at control he was exerting and it worried her. It had been like kissing a block of tempered steel, cold and hard and unresponsive.

What's wrong? She had opened her lips to form the words but Cal spoke first.

'There's something I want to ask you', he said abruptly.

'Ask away!' No, that airy tone had been a mistake, Helen realised, noting the swift, dark frown that crossed Cal's face at her light-hearted response, the sight of it starting up the erratic pulsing of her heart once more so that she felt a pounding in her temples making a sound like the roar of thunder echo inside her head.

So the moment had come, and in one way she was glad of it, feeling unable to cope with the uncertainty of not knowing for very much longer—but in another she was afraid of what was coming, not feeling at all ready. Because in the few minutes since she had come back into the house she had been intensely aware of Cal as never before. It was as if the distance he had put between them had enabled her to take a step backwards, see him more clearly, and what she saw had a devastating effect on her emotions.

She had thought that it was impossible to be more aware of Cal than she had been last night with every instinct heightened by anticipation, the excitement of discovery, but now she found that there was a very different and much more sensual impact that came from seeing him for the first time with the full knowledge of his lovemaking locked deep in her heart. Never before had his hair appeared so golden, the glint of copper in it more pronounced in the light of the lamp on the table beside him, his eyes gleaming jewel-bright as he sprawled in his chair, those long legs stretched out in front of him.

'What was it you wanted to know?' she prompted uncertainly as Cal still remained silent.

The frown that creased his forehead darkened ominously as he set down his glass with unnecessarily meticulous care.

'About last night,' he said slowly, then suddenly the green eyes swung round to her face, locking with her grey ones and holding her gaze with a hypnotic intensity. 'Who did you did you sleep with last night, Helen?' he demanded harshly.

The question did not make sense. 'Who?' Helen echoed dazedly. What did he mean? What *could* he mean? 'I—don't understand,' she said shakily. 'That's a crazy question.'

'It's a perfectly resonable question, and one I have to know the answer to,' Cal snapped. His eyes had lost all trace of warmth, they were just emerald splinters of ice in his tightly drawn face. 'So tell me, Helen, who did you make love with last night—Jay Keller or Cal Hyde?'

'Jay——' Helen began, then broke off abruptly as Cal pushed himself from his chair with a violent movement and swung away from her to stand staring out of the window, his shoulders hunched and his hands pushed deep into his trouser pockets. Fear dried Helen's throat. What had she said to provoke such a reaction in him? 'Cal——' she tried again, her voice just a painful croak. 'Please——'

Very slowly he turned back to her and the sight of his face made her heart twist deep inside her. His cheek and jaw muscles were rigid with tension, his expression turned to stone, and that rigidity was echoed in his body too, it was stiff and taut as if he was holding himself away from her.

'Answer me!' he said in a voice made all the more compelling by its unnatural quietness, sending shivers of dread like the trickle of cold water down Helen's spine just to hear it. Doctor Jekyll had vanished completely; Mr Hyde was well and truly back in control.

'Jay Keller—Cal Hyde——' Helen stumbled over the words. 'They're one and the same person, so what does it matter? They're both you.'

'Are they?'

In a catalogue of unexpected questions, this one was the most surprising and the most shocking. Helen could only stare at Cal's hardened face, blank amazement and sheer incredulity making her eyes just wide, dark pools above her ashen cheeks.

'*Are they?*' Cal repeated his question savagely.

'Of—of course they are! You're Cal—you told me Keller was just a stage name, I know that.' Helen could hardly believe that the voice she was hearing was her own. It came and went with a crazy unevenness, high-pitched and sharp with nerves at first then sinking to a despairing whisper. 'But you're Jay Keller, too.'

'No, I'm not.'

Those three sharp words lashed out at Helen with the force of a whip and she felt their impact like physical blows. *No, I'm not.* Could she possibly have heard him right? Was that really what he had said? She couldn't believe it was true, and in the stunned silence that followed she slowly shook her head in disbelief, wanting to deny that she had ever heard him speak.

'I'm not Jay Keller, Helen,' Cal repeated slowly and emphatically, his words barely impinging on the grey fog that clouded her mind, preventing her from thinking clearly.

'Don't be ridiculous!' She winced to hear the words come out so harsh and shrill. 'Of course you're——'

She broke off abruptly as Cal shook his head adamantly, his green eyes probing deep into hers as if searching into the depths of her mind, willing her to believe him.

'And—Cal Hyde?' she asked tremulously.

Cal's laugh was short and hard. 'Oh, I'm Cal all right. Cal Hyde's the name I was given at birth, the only name I've any claim to. But Jay Keller is someone else entirely.'

'Who?' It was just a thin thread of sound, but Cal caught it.

'Joel,' he said soberly.

'Joel? Your brother?'

'My brother,' Cal confirmed sardonically. 'My identical twin brother, to be exact.'

His *twin*! Helen had thought it was impossible her bruised mind could take any further shocks, but now it seemed that her brain was so numb from the blows it had already received it could only accept this last fact without any reaction, almost as if it had been inevitable. But even as she accepted Cal's words she was struggling to adjust to the implications behind them. *Joel*—'My brother'— 'As a matter of fact, he was the one who made up the stage name'. From two days before, the memory of what Cal had said drifted back to her.

'You lied to me!' It was a low moan of pain, but as she uttered the words a blazing fire of anger swept through Helen, driving the misery before it. 'You *lied* to me!' she cried on a completely different note.

'No!' Cal's tone was sharp. 'I never really lied to you, Helen. I just let you go on believing I was Jay. That was what you wanted to believe and I could see no reason for disillusioning you—until last night.'

Last night. The words stopped Helen dead in her tracks. In her shock at Cal's revelation she had forgotten about last night, but now the memory came rushing back with a force that made her head reel so violently she felt she might almost lose consciousness. Last night had been a lie from start to finish! She had given herself to this man, believing he was someone else. His loving had been as false as that damned butterfly—which now, too late, she realised wasn't false at all, but was etched on the skin of another man.

'I did try to tell you,' Cal put in almost as if he could read her mind. 'I said we had to talk.'

'So you did.' Helen spoke through lips that were unnaturally stiff with the effort of holding back emotions that threatened to break through her control. If she once let them free they would swamp her like some tidal wave destroying everything in its path.

'But you——'

'I know what I did!' She didn't want to be reminded of how stupid she had been, didn't want to recall how the fire of passion had burned her up so that she had been oblivious to any possible repercussions, had silenced his attempts to explain with those foolish words 'Let's just let our bodies do the talking', blotting out the voice of reason or self-preservation so that in the end she had only herself to blame for the predicament she now found herself in. But she couldn't take all the blame. Cal had had plenty of other opportunities to explain.

'But I also know what you did!' she declared, a note of anger ringing in her voice. 'You deceived me right from the start. You deceived all of us, letting us believe you were Jay Keller—even at the party.'

'I know.' Cal pushed an impatient hand through his hair, ruffling its bright sleekness so that now, when she was least able to handle it, he looked even more like the Jay Keller she had seen on that television show, aeons ago it seemed. 'But that was just chance. I was doing Joel a favour. He had to get away early, he had an important recording session in London coming up and he needed a break. It's a trick we often played when we were kids— our parents were the only ones who could tell us apart— and under ordinary circumstances it would all have passed off without comment, with no one being any the wiser; it was just a twist of fate that this time it became rather more than that. I wasn't to know you'd chosen that particular night to carry out your stunt of kidnapping Jay Keller—not knowing you'd got the wrong man.'

'But you could have told me later—on that first morning.'

Cal's smile was wry. 'I was in no mood to tell anyone

anything that morning.' A hard edge crept into his voice. 'I was angry, furious at the way I'd been treated, at the loss of my freedom and the cavalier fashion in which the whole business had been carried out. You want to try being doped and carted off God knows where.' Helen flinched at the sardonic bite of Cal's words. 'Believe me, it doesn't exactly make for a calm or rational frame of mind.'

'No,' Helen murmured, not looking at him, afraid to meet his eyes for fear she might see now some of the anger he had felt then. Hadn't she seen the suppressed fury, the barely controlled frustration burning in him on that first morning—and sympathised with it? 'I wasn't very happy about that myself,' she admitted in a low voice.

'I know. That was the first thing I realised when I started thinking rationally again. Then, when I talked to you, I realised you had the very best of reasons for going along with Ricky's plan and that Ricky's motives too had been very honourable, even if I didn't like the way he'd gone about things. I began to get involved, to care about your fund-raising effort—all the more so when I learned about your sister. But I still couldn't tell you—well, for two reasons really. One is that Joel and I have this arrangement. He's never told anyone about me or the farm and I've never admitted that he's my brother. That way we both get a little peace—I'm spared the sightseers and reporters trailing all over the farm, disrupting everything, and Joel has somewhere he can come home to when he needs a break from all the publicity he has to endure. We've worked things like that from the beginning when he first started out, and although it's been hellishly difficult at times to keep things from the media, in general it's worked pretty well—until now. But I couldn't just tell you how things were—it was Joel's secret too, not just mine.'

Once more Cal pushed his hand through his hair, his green eyes intent on Helen's face.

'And as for the second reason—well, you thought you'd kidnapped Jay Keller, that he could make the contribution to the funds you so wanted. I thought it was better to let you continue believing I was Jay rather than disillusion you.'

Cal paused and now, at last, Helen found the strength to lift her eyes to his, seeing in them not the anger she had expected, but an open, direct honesty, the force of which willed her to believe every word he was saying.

'I thought you'd be devastated if you discovered you'd got the wrong man. Was I mistaken?'

'No.' Helen shook her head slowly. He had not been mistaken, his assessment of how she might have felt was disturbingly accurate. She had had ambiguous feelings about the whole stunt from the beginning, if she had known that the man they had kidnapped was not Jay Keller at all but his brother, someone completely separate from the famous rock star, she would never have been able to handle it. 'No,' she repeated, her voice low, 'you weren't wrong at all.'

Cal's sigh was a sound of relief. 'I thought so. That's why I decided to wait until Ricky got back, that and another reason we won't go into now. I thought it would be better to explain the whole situation to him. But I'll admit that, at first, I wanted to teach you a lesson. I wanted to show you that you can't just mess around with other people's lives, for whatever reason, without facing up to the consequences. I still want to impress that fact on your brother,' he added a trifle grimly.

'So what made you change your mind?' Helen felt she already knew the answer, but the question still had to be asked.

'I don't really have to explain that, do I? I should have thought it was perfectly obvious. I hadn't anticipated certain—developments—and by the time I realised which way the wind was blowing things were happening so fast I wasn't quite ready for them.'

And that Helen could believe. She had been as unprepared as Cal for the blazing passion that had taken fire between them on the previous night, sweeping aside all thought of restraint or caution. She had only known that she had wanted to go along with it, experience it, live it to the fullest, so much so that now, when it had suddenly turned sour on her, she felt desolate and mentally bruised by the shock.

'Who *are* you?' The words came stiffly through lips clamped tight against the floodtide of her feelings. 'I mean, who are you really? Who is Cal Hyde?'

Cal's smile was slow and gentle. 'A farmer,' he said softly, the smile widening at her start of surprise.

'In Yorkshire?' Cal would never know what made her voice so shaken and uneven. He knew nothing of her private dream, of the secret longing that Cal could be not Jay Keller, but just a farmer like his father in the childhood he had described so vividly. Now she had her wish, but it had rebounded on her with a bitter irony so that she no longer knew if it was what she wanted or not.

'In Yorkshire,' Cal confirmed. 'Joel and I inherited my father's farm when he died, but he didn't have a spark of interest in running the place—he's always been much more the big-city type—so eventually I bought him out. By then, of course, his singing career had taken off and now he rarely even visits the place. So you see, everything I told you about the farm, my childhood—it was all the truth. Apart from that one omission at the beginning, I have been honest with you, Helen.'

There was a note of conviction in his tone, one that begged her to believe what he said. She *wanted* to believe him—but could she?

Helen found she could not take her eyes from the man before her. He was Cal and yet not Cal, not as she had believed she knew him. He was the same, heartbreakingly, tormentingly the same, and yet so very, very different., Those stunning looks, the strong lines of his body, still had the power to draw her like a magnet. Just to look at him set her heart pounding, drying her mouth with a burning awareness of the sensual impact of his physical presence. Did it matter if he wasn't the man she had thought he was? Her body declared that none of that mattered at all, but her mind could not agree. She had been caught by deceit before, caught and betrayed.

'Helen?' Cal's voice was hesitant, questioning, and Helen knew the question was one she wasn't ready to answer.

'You said there was another reason for your staying,' she said jerkily, her voice betraying her inner turmoil. 'What was that?'

The slow smile that spread across his face made her breath catch in her throat, her heart seeming to stand still for a second then jolt back into action faster than before.

'Oh, Helen,' Cal said softly. 'Do you really not know?'

Every instinct told her what he was going to say. It was there in the light in his eyes, in that smile. But even as she acknowledged that, she knew her mind was willing her to reject it, to deny what was coming, because she didn't want to hear it. She didn't know how to handle it.

'No!' It was barely a whisper and her hands came up before her face in a shaky, defensive gesture. Please, let him not say that!

'But you must know, Helen,' Cal continued inexor-

ably. 'The real reason I stayed was you. The more I saw of
you, the more I wanted to get to know you. I wanted to
take it slowly, find out all about you, and most of all I
wanted you to know the truth about me before I made
any moves, but it didn't exactly work out that way.
Helen, what I'm trying to say is that I love you.'

'No!' The moaning cry escaped involuntarily. She
didn't want this, had had no thought of love when she
had admitted how attracted she was to Cal. Loving
brought complications like pain and betrayal and she
wasn't prepared to risk those feelings again.

'Yes.' Cal's voice was softly insistent. 'I love you,
Helen. I fell in love with you the first moment I saw
you—or if not then, then in the garden a few minutes
later. You can call it the effect of the moonlight if you
like, but all I know is that I've never felt like that before
about anyone. I knew then you were the girl I wanted to
marry.'

It was uncanny, it was frightening how closely his
words echoed David's, mirroring them almost exactly,
reviving all the hurt and anguish she had tried so hard to
bury in the last twelve months. 'I knew from the moment
I saw you that you were the girl I wanted to marry.'
David had said that too, and in her naïve gullibilty she
had believed him, had given her heart without reserva-
tion, only to have it torn into little pieces. Never again.
She knew better now.

'I told you that you're the most beautiful woman I've
ever seen——'

'No!' Helen's sharp cry tore through the air as she
sprang to her feet, her eyes dark with pain in an ashen
face. 'No! No! No!'

David had said that too, had told her that she was the
most beautiful woman, the *only* woman for him, and all

the time he had been lying, lying to himself as well as to her, his thoughts far away even then, far away with some other woman, the one he had really loved.

'I don't want this, Cal! I don't want your love—I don't believe in it. It isn't real. It isn't true!'

Cal took a step backwards, his face changing, becoming rigid with shock. He looked as if a door had slammed shut in his face so that, just for a second, Helen wondered—but just as swiftly squashed the weak thought down again. How could he love her when he had deceived her in this way?

'I don't believe you!' she cried again. 'No, don't touch me!' as he made a move towards her, lifting his hand as if he would have caught hold of her arm.

Suddenly all she wanted was to be free of him, to have him go and leave her in peace, though she doubted if there would ever be any peace for her now that those dark memories which she had hoped, had believed were long buried had resurfaced so shatteringly. Somehow Cal had unlocked her own private Pandora's box of the past, letting those black, unhappy images fly free once again.

'Helen——' Cal began, but Helen broke in on him sharply, wanting to be rid of him, to see him walk out of the door and leave her alone.

'Leave me alone!' Her voice was shrill in the quiet room. 'Just go away and leave me alone!' What did she have to do to make him go? And then suddenly she knew just what to say, knew exactly what would make him leave once and for all. 'I don't want you!' she sobbed. 'I never did. I thought you were Jay Keller. I don't know who Cal Hyde is, but——'

But she didn't have to go any further. Cal's face closed against her, the light dying from his eyes, leaving them as bleak and cold as a winter sea.

'I see,' he said harshly. 'So that's the way it is.'

'Yes.' Ruthlessly Helen pushed home her advantage. 'Yes, that's the way it is. So now will you please go? I don't want you here, I never did. Just go and get out of my life—I never want to see you again.'

In the end she was speaking to an empty room. Without another word Cal had turned on his heel and stalked out, leaving her standing stiffly alone. With her arms wrapped tightly around her body as she struggled to regain control of her emotions, Helen heard the faint sound of his movements in the bedroom as he collected his few belongings and minutes later his footsteps descended the stairs once more. Only when she heard the front door bang behind him and knew that he had gone did she allow herself to move, taking the few unsteady steps that brought her to the safety of an armchair into which she sank down thankfully, her whole body trembling with reaction.

CHAPTER SEVEN

'WELL? What happened?'

The sight of Ricky's smiling, cheerful face was almost more than Helen could take when he strolled into the house late on Saturday evening. From the very start nothing had gone right for her that day and the fact that she had hardly slept at all the night before did little to improve her mood. The appearance of her brother, looking relaxed, healthy and positively glowing with delight at the triumph of having completed the sponsored walk in record time, and clearly only too keen to hear every detail of the time she had spent with Jay Keller, was definitely the last straw.

'It's about time you put in an appearance,' she snapped, as much to give herself time, put off the moment she knew had to come, as from any real sense of irritation. 'I've done nothing but take telephone messages for you all day long. Everyone in the world seems to want to contact you.'

She knew she sounded bitchy and she regretted the words as soon as they had left her mouth. It wasn't the number of phone calls that had upset her, but the fact that every time the telephone had rung her heart had lurched painfully at the irrational thought that perhaps Cal might try to contact her. It had done no good to tell herself that he would never do any such thing, that the angry words she had flung at him must have driven him away for good, and it had been equally unhelpful to try to convince herself that the last thing she wanted was to hear from Cal Hyde after the way he had treated her. No matter what arguments she used to persuade herself, it was still Cal's face she pictured as she lifted the receiver, Cal's voice she expected to hear, so that it came as a jolting shock when someone else, usually female, asked to speak to her brother.

The anticipatory light faded from Ricky's eyes and he frowned at Helen's uncharacteristic petulance.

'What's wrong, Sis?' he asked. 'Didn't you get on with Jay Keller?'

Just how did she answer that? Ricky was no fool, he would know if she was lying, he would read it in her face. She knew she had already caught his attention by her start when he spoke that name, one that sounded strangely alien to her now after days of thinking of Cal by his proper name—and Jay Keller was someone else entirely. Deciding honesty—or part honesty at least— was the best policy, she said awkwardly, 'He wasn't exactly as I expected him to be.'

'But then you were prejudiced against him to begin with,' Ricky reminded her cheefully. 'I thought he seemed a reasonable enough sort of fellow. Tell me,' he added disconcertingly, 'was it Jay in particular or just any man? I know Bentley messed you about, but really, Sis, you're far too young to become a man-hater for life. You can't let one bad experience sour you for ever.'

'I think "bad experience" is an understatement, Ricky!'

Helen didn't know whether to be angry or relieved that her brother had veered off on to this particular track. It distracted him from talking about Cal, but she found his comments very disturbing indeed.

'David ruined my life.' And Ricky only knew half of it, she admitted to herself, for she had never been able to bring herself to tell anyone the true reason for his jilting her as he had done. 'And I'm not soured—just cautious.'

'Cautious!' Ricky's snort was a sound of disgusted incredulity. 'Come off it, Nell! You've been avoiding any contact with men ever since. I told you—it's time you started living again. You have to loosen up.'

'Loosen up!' The sharpness of Helen's tone betrayed the way she was feeling. Her cheeks had lost their pallor; they were suddenly burning hot. She hadn't been cautious with Cal—she had 'loosened up' then—and look where it had got her! Right back to the beginning with only pain and lies and deceit to show for her attempt at 'starting living again'. If that was living she preferred not to try it. 'Ricky, I really don't think this is any business of yours—it's my life.'

'So it is.' Ricky dismissed her argument with a wave of his hand. 'But you're making a real mess of it, Nell. You're a young woman, a good-looking woman too, it's not right that you should lock yourself away like this.'

Helen barely heard the latter half of Ricky's speech. His first words had brought a memory springing to the surface of her mind, the recollection of something Cal had said on that very first day.

'Which mess, Helen?' he had asked. 'The glass on the floor or the mess you're making of your life?' and remembering the softly intent tone in which those words had been spoken Helen felt the heat leave her cheeks in a rush as she shivered in reaction, then caught herself up as the slight action drew Ricky's eyes to her.

'It's turned chilly, hasn't it?' she offered as an excuse for the tremor that had shaken her, but even in her own ears her voice didn't sound terribly convincing, sliding out of control so that it came out high-pitched and uneven. 'I—I think I'll just go and get a cardigan.'

She escaped upstairs before Ricky could say another word to hold her back.

It took only a minute to reach her room, but another five to control her unsteady breathing and the pounding heartbeat that had been her reaction to that unwanted memory. At last the frantic racing stopped and Helen sank down on her bed feeling weak and exhausted, but at least her mind was now clear of the hazy mist that had filled it. She had to think, had to decide what she was going to tell Ricky—because she had to tell him something. He would want to know about the ransom. After the way she had spoken to him on the phone earlier in the week, he had come home confident that things had gone well, fully expecting her to hand over the money Jay Keller—for he still believed that Jay was the man they had kidnapped—had paid as the price of his release.

How was she going to explain to him that there was no money? She couldn't tell him the reasons for that without giving away everything that had happened and her own part in sending Cal away. She hadn't thought of the money then, hadn't thought of anything beyond getting him out of the house and out of her life. Helen sighed despondently. She had thought it was impossible for her to feel any more miserable than she did already, but this final realisation made her spirits sink so low she thought they would never rise again. The only reason she had gone along with Ricky's scheme in the first place was her desire, fired by the memory of Trish's short, sad life, to do something to ensure that other children in the same situation could be helped. Now it seemed that in that she had failed, too.

Drawing herself up, Helen squared her shoulders resolutely. She couldn't put this off a moment longer. She was going to have to explain to Ricky that there was no money and she had better get it done now. If she was lucky she might be able to get away with avoiding explaining the real reasons why the ransom hadn't been paid.

On her way downstairs she paused outside the door to the spare bedroom, her mind going irresistibly to the night she had spent there with Cal. As if of its own volition her hand reached out and touched the door, pushing it open slightly. She would just take one look, she told herself. That might convince her that Cal had gone and then perhaps she would be free of these restless, unsettled feelings.

The envelope was the first thing that caught her eye. Lying on the dressing-table, it was the one thing out of place in the otherwise immaculately tidy room, its white colour standing out sharply against the polished wood. As if in a dream she crossed the room to pick it up.

What had she expected? Some letter to herself, an apology perhaps? Helen couldn't be sure if she had actually hoped for some such thing, she only knew the uncomfortable twisting sensation deep in her stomach when she saw the name Richard Seymour inscribed across the envelope in a firm, clear hand.

For a long moment she held the letter slightly away from her, as if afraid it might grow teeth and bite. What had Cal written to Ricky about? How much had he told him? With a nervous shudder she remembered the cold anger burning in Cal on that first morning when he had woken in this very room. Had that anger, that determination to point out to her brother how misjudged his actions had been, resurfaced in the last minutes before he left the house so that he had written this letter telling Ricky everything? And how much was everything? There was only one way to find out. Drawing a deep breath she took the letter downstairs to her brother.

'What's this?' Ricky eyed the sealed envelope curiously.

'Open it and see.' Helen could not suppress the tautness in her voice, her heart seemed to be beating high up in her throat as Ricky ripped open the envelope and extracted the single sheet of paper enclosed within it.

It was too small to be a letter, Helen noted hazily, barely registering her brother's exclamation of delight that changed so swiftly to a sound of surprise and confusion.

'Who's this Calder Hyde?' he demanded abruptly and the name sounded so strange on his lips that for a moment Helen could only stare in blank incomprehension. Then realisation dawned and she adjusted her expression swiftly.

'Oh—Jay Keller's just a stage name. What—what is it, Ricky?' she asked, not at all sure she wanted to know.

'A cheque.' Ricky waved the slip of paper under her nose.' A wonderful, magnificent cheque made out to the Kidney Unit fund. A cheque—wait for it——' he paused dramatically '—for twice the amount we asked.'

'Ohhh.'

It was all Helen could manage. This was the last thing she had expected. After the way she and Cal had parted she had convinced herself that she had ruined any chance of his making a contribution to the Rag appeal, and now to find that not only had he done so but that he had actually paid more than the required ransom made her feel as if the ground was crumbling away beneath her feet, becoming too insubstantial to support her.

The next moment she gasped in shock as Ricky's arms came round her, snatching her up in an enveloping hug and swinging her off her feet. The room blurred before her eyes. It was as if she had entered a time-slip, going back forty-eight hours in the space of a second, so that for a moment she imagined Ricky's arms were Cal's around her when he had gathered her close, the memory so vivid that it rocked her sense of reality, and when Ricky finally set her back on her feet she found she was trembling with shock, her grey eyes wide and dark in an ashen face.

'Helen, you're a wonder!' Ricky clearly hadn't noticed her distress. 'I don't know what you did to him but whatever it was it worked—but then I told you it would. I know you had your doubts, but they can't matter now. It's all been wonderfully worth while, hasn't it?—Helen?' At last his sister's silence seemed to penetrate the euphoria that gripped him. 'Hasn't it?' he repeated less confidently.

Unable to meet his eyes for fear he might read something of what she was feeling in her own, Helen forced a smile.

'Yes,' she assured him, careful control making her voice as steady as she could have wished. 'Yes, it's been well worth while.'

For the Kidney Unit at least, she added silently to herself, unable to prevent herself from thinking of the cost to herself of the whole enterprise and wondering if, in personal terms, that cost had been way, way too high.

That thought returned to plague her again and again

during the next twenty-four hours. She was unable to put
Cal out of her mind, the deliberate way he had deceived
her warring with her acknowledgement of his generosity
and thoughtfulness in making such a substantial donation to the charity that meant so much to her, in spite of
all that had happened between them, until she felt she
would never again acquire a mental balance where Cal
Hyde was concerned. The constant veering back and
forth of her opinion of him made her fractious and ill-
tempered, quite unlike her usual calm, controlled self,
and she knew that Ricky saw the change in her and that
it bothered him. He tolerated her swift changes of mood
for a time, but by Sunday evening he had had enough.

'OK, Sis, what is it?' he demanded at last. 'You've
been like a bear with a sore head all day and I want to
know why. What's bugging you? Is it something I've
done?'

'Yes—no——'

Helen didn't know how to answer him. It would be
easy enough to say yes, it was all his fault. If he hadn't
thought up the plan of kidnapping Jay Keller in the first
place, if he hadn't cleared off on his sponsored walk
leaving her and Cal alone in the house, then none of this
might have happened. But she knew that to say that was
not being completely honest.

No one had made her decisions for her. She had
chosen to let Cal make love to her, in fact she had
actively encouraged him. She felt hot and then shiveringly cold at the memory of her actions on that night, at
the thought of the way she had stopped Cal when he had
tried to explain the truth to her—and he *had* tried. In the
cold light of day, without her perception clouded by
anger, she could see that now, and the realisation made

her own ambiguous, changeable feelings all the harder to bear.

'No,' she said quietly but more firmly. 'No, Ricky, it's nothing you've done.'

'Then what is it?' Ricky leaned towards her, his eyes dark with concern. 'You haven't been yourself ever since I arrived home yesterday. What's caused this? Is it something to do with Jay Keller? I'm not blind,' he added, hearing Helen's choked gasp. 'I've seen how you jump like a startled cat whenever his name's mentioned, and you were definitely cagey over the phone when I rang up during the week. So what is it, Nell? Is it anything I can help with?'

If he hadn't already half guessed, if he hadn't been so obviously concerned, she might have managed to fob him off with some story of not feeling too well, but his words breached the barriers in her mind and, before she quite realised it was happening, the whole story had come pouring out, garbled and disjointed in places, as she stumbled over bits that were hard to express.

And all the time she was speaking she had a vividly clear image of Cal in her mind, her thoughts picturing the clear, bright colour of his hair, the long, strong hands, the firm, shapely lines of his body, and above all else the intent emerald brightness of those vivid green eyes, and the look in them when she had told him to go, that she didn't want him, that she had only ever wanted Jay Keller, not Cal Hyde.

It was as she spoke those dreadful words out loud to Ricky, seeing her brother's quick frown in response, that she knew finally and without any hope of redemption that the things she had said had been a lie. She had wanted *Cal* from the moment she had first set eyes on him and she still wanted him now, in spite of everything that had happened. Who or what he was didn't matter.

'Phew!' Ricky let his breath out in a long, reflective sigh. 'We certainly messed things up between us, didn't we? Nell, I swear to you I had no idea that we'd got the wrong man. I didn't even know there *was* a brother. I'd never have gone through with it if I'd so much as suspected——'

'It's all right,' Helen broke in on him, smiling a little sadly at the forcefulness of his words. 'I understand that, Ricky, you don't have to explain. You didn't know, no one knew——' Her voice broke on the words. No one had known, except Cal, and he had kept that information to himself.

'Tell me something, Sis.' Ricky's boyish face looked uncharacteristically serious, his sombre expression adding years to his face, making him look so much older. 'Did Jay—I mean Cal——' He hesitated, then, apparently coming to a decision, continued more firmly. 'Did he remind you of David at all?'

Frankly startled by the question, Helen nevertheless gave it serious and honest consideration.

'I don't think so,' she said slowly, then shook her head. 'No,' she continued definitely, 'he wasn't like David at all in himself, he couldn't have been more different in many ways, but——'

'But?' Ricky pressed her when she broke off to consider the thought that had surfaced in her head.

'He—made me think of David a lot just by being here, revived memories I've tried to forget, things I wanted to bury when David jilted me. I suppose it was inevitable really, there's been no other man here since then.'

'I see.' Ricky nodded his understanding. 'And when

you—I'm sorry, Sis, but I have to say this—when you slept with him——'

If she hadn't been well aware of how serious he was being, how much importance he placed on the things he was saying, Helen might have found Ricky's boyishly embarrassed expression rather comical.

'Go on,' she told him. 'Say what you mean. I can take it.'

And suddenly she knew she could take whatever Ricky was about to say. It might hurt, it might even devastate her, she was sure it was going to rock some of her long-held assumptions about herself, but every instinct told her that it had to be done if she was ever going to clarify the muddled feelings that had tormented her since Cal's departure—no, for longer than that. She had been on this emotional see-saw since that moment in the college gardens when Cal had first taken her into his arms. If she was ever going to sort out just what she did or did not feel then she had to face up to a few home truths of the sort she suspected Ricky was about to hand her now.

'All right.' Ricky took a deep breath and plunged on. 'When you and Cal made love, did you think of David then?'

'Oh, no!' Helen's response was swift and vehement. She had had no thought of anyone else when Cal had made love to her, had been incapable of thinking of anything beyond the pleasure of the touch of his hands, the pressure of his lips on hers. No memory of David had marred the wonder of those moments.

Cal had been no substitute for anyone. She hadn't been transferring longings for another man on to him. Helen's mouth twisted bitterly. She could never have lived with herself if she had done that. Hadn't that been what

David had done to her? And she had been so totally destroyed when she had found out.

'No, Ricky,' she admitted honestly, all embarrassment at talking to her younger brother in this way vanishing before the need to express the truth. 'It was Cal I wanted, only Cal and no one else, and—and——' Grey eyes opened wide in shock as she realised the enormity of what she was about to say, her mind reeling as if from a blow so that she had to force herself to continue. 'And I don't regret it for one minute.'

There was no denying the ring of sincerity in her voice and she could tell from the way Ricky's head went back that he was as startled to hear it as she was herself.

'So why did you send him away?' he demanded bluntly.

'Ricky—he lied to me!'

'He didn't want to,' Ricky pointed out with what Helen felt was a streak of ruthlessness she hadn't seen in him before. 'Except at the beginning, and you've got to understand that when you consider the pretty mean trick we'd played on him. You told me yourself that *you* stopped him when he tried to tell you. Nell, you've admitted that you wanted him, that you don't regret making love with him, so *why* did you send him away?'

'I—don't know,' Helen admitted shakily, her head bent.

'Well, I do.' A faint smile touched Ricky's mouth at the way his sister's head came up swiftly in surprise. 'And so will you if you'll only think and admit what you were really feeling. Cal told you he loved you.'

'Yes.' Helen's mind was too numbed, too bruised to manage more than the single syllable.

'And you couldn't handle it—that's why you told him to go.'

'*Couldn't handle it!* Ricky, what are you trying to say?'

'Oh, Nell!'

Ricky leaned forward and took her hand in his. It seemed to Helen as if the years that separated them had suddenly dwindled to nothing, as if their positions had been reversed, she thought bemusedly. Here was her younger, often teasingly tolerated brother taking on the role of the older sibling, offering advice and comfort as she had done for him many times before. Strangely enough, she found the reversal of roles very comforting.

'Think about it,' Ricky was saying. 'Remember the day David jilted you—the day that should have been your wedding day. No, don't dodge away,' he put in hurriedly, seeing the way Helen flinched and stiffened at his words. 'You have to remember it, Nell, for your own good. You have to go back if you're ever to go forwards.'

Remember your wedding day. A sharp shaft of pain ripped through Helen and she wanted to tear her hands from Ricky's, spring to her feet and flee from the room. She didn't want to remember. But her brother's blue eyes were steady on her face, willing her to trust him, so she bit down on her bottom lip hard to stop its trembling, using the small physical hurt as a counterbalance to her mental anguish, and nodded shakily.

'Remember when the telegram came.' Ricky's voice was low but firm and Helen pictured in her mind the house bright with spring sunshine, much as her own home was today, the bustle of preparations, the scent of the perfumed bath from which she had just emerged—a perfume which had once been her favourite, but which now she could never smell without feeling physically sick. There had been a ring at the doorbell and her mother, lightly declaring that there was no peace for the wicked, had gone to answer it.

'Mother had hysterics,' she said in a small voice.

'Didn't she just,' Ricky agreed, his eyes lighting with what she realised with some surprise was compassion. She had thought that, being a man, her brother could never understand the way she had felt that day, but it seemed she had been wrong. 'If there was anyone who was entitled to go to pieces it was you—but did you? No.' He shook his head firmly as he answered his own question. 'Mother had the hysterics. You just went white—just for a minute. I remember you said, "There isn't going to be a wedding. David's changed his mind." And then, almost in the same breath, you began talking about going to the church to tell everyone. You said the presents would have to be sent back, the reception cancelled. You talked about anything except how you *felt*.'

'Those things had to be done!' Helen couldn't see what point Ricky was trying to make. 'Someone had to do them.'

'But it didn't have to be *you*. Look, Nell, you've always been the oldest, the sensible one—my responsible big sister. I suppose a lot of it comes from Trish being so ill. You were only eleven when they found out how sick she was and suddenly you had to grow up—fast. Mother needed help, Trish needed help, and there you were. I can remember you getting home from school and setting to to cook a meal before you'd even think about your homework or the telly or any of the normal things kids want to do. You took Mum's place when she had to be in the hospital with Trish, and we all came to rely on you to keep the home running while she was away. Perhaps we relied on you too much. You were always there, always ready to put someone else first, before your own needs. It was only when Trish died that you were free to do as you wanted. That's true, isn't it?'

'Yes.'

Helen's voice was just a whisper. She was remembering how, at twenty, she had suddenly realised that her mother and father didn't need her help any more and that Ricky, at fifteen, was more than capable of looking after himself, no longer needing his older sister to act as subsitute mother when he came home from school. That was when she had applied for the job at Frazer and Crown and had moved to the city in order to take it up—a move that had resulted in her meeting with David when he had come in to enquire about a flat that had just come on to the estate agents' books.

'But I don't see what this has to do with Cal,' she said uncertainly.

'I'm coming to that. Look, Nell, what I'm trying to say is that from when you were very young you were trained to be responsible, to put others first, and you've always done that. I remember you first took an interest in Bentley because he needed your help. You said he seemed lost and alone.'

And that, too, was true. There had been an air of sadness about David, a bruised, hurt look in his eyes that had drawn her sympathy. It had been a long time before she had persuaded him to tell her the reasons for it and by then it was too late—she had already fallen in love with him.

'It wasn't just that I want to help him,' she protested, and Ricky nodded understandingly.

'I know, but that was part of it. And when he jilted you—at a time when anyone could have been forgiven for blowing their top and going completely to pieces—did you? No, not sensible, responsible Helen. You were the one who took charge, the one who went to the church and told everyone the wedding was off, *you* cancelled the reception, supervised the return of the presents—thinking of everyone else, not yourself. And when it was all over you took yourself back to this house and went into work as if nothing had happened. You didn't even take a single day off.'

'There was no need to! The leave I'd taken was to have been for—for the honeymoon. There was no point in using it just to sit about at home moping.'

'No?' Ricky's question was soft, but it pierced like an arrow, because at last Helen was beginning to understand where this was all leading. 'What about mourning time, Helen? What about time to let yourself go, admit that you'd been hurt, to cry, to break down that careful control you'd built around yourself, and acknowledge you needed help? What about that, Helen?'

'Perhaps I didn't need it.' There was no conviction in Helen's voice. She was well aware of the way Ricky had used her full name instead of his usual casual nickname, that small fact indicative of just how serious he was being.

'Rubbish! Everyone needs time like that after a bereavement—and losing David in that way was as much a bereavement to you as if he'd died. You needed to mourn your loss, Helen, everyone has to do that or they don't heal. You never did mourn David and I don't believe you've ever properly recovered from what he did to you.'

'You can't hide away with a broken heart for ever.' It was such a short time since Ricky had said those words to her and she had denied them angrily, but now she was not so sure. She hadn't been able to talk to Cal about David, not properly. She had turned away his compliments because they had reminded her of the times David had called her beautiful, and—yes, oh God, it was true—she had driven him away not because he hadn't told her the truth, she could understand that now and she knew only too well that he *had* tried to tell her and she had prevented him from doing so. No, that had only been an excuse made up in order to avoid facing up to the real reason why she had rejected him.

Cal had said that he loved her and those words had provoked such a reaction of fear and blind panic because, as Ricky had said, she still wasn't healed from the pain David had inflicted on her. She hadn't wanted to risk having anything to do with love again because her first experience of that emotion had ended in such disaster.

And Ricky had been right in another thing too. She *hadn't* had time to mourn her loss, she had turned in on herself, enclosing her feelings inside thick, strong walls that she had believed shut out all the hurt and the anger, but in fact had kept them inside her, growing and festering over the past twelve months. When she had cried out to Cal that she didn't want him, that she had never wanted him, it had not been *Cal* she had wanted to hurt but *David*! She remembered thinking that somehow Cal had managed to unlock the Pandora's box of her past, but only now, too late, did she realise how close to the truth she had been. He had opened up the buried memories and the harsh words she had flung at him had

been directed not at him, but at the man who had jilted
her: all the anger and pain she had wanted and needed to
pour out twelve months before and had been unable to do
so because David had not had the courage to face her
himself. He had sent her the telegram as he left for the
station on his way to take up a new job in Glasgow and by
the time his letter arrived he was hundreds of miles away.

'Oh, Ricky!' Hot tears of remorse burned in Helen's
eyes as she turned to her brother. 'What *am* I going to
do?'

'That depends on what you want to do.' Ricky was not
going to make things easy for her.' How do you feel about
Cal now—now that you know the truth?'

How *did* she feel? Once more an image of Cal's face
floated before Helen's inner eye, not the hard, angry Mr
Hyde of the first day after the kidnapping, but the warm,
gentle man who had understood her sorrow when she
talked of Trish, the man who had said he was honoured
to be part of the scheme to help the Kidney Unit, who in
spite of everything she had said had still left that cheque
for twice the amount Ricky had asked, the man she had
fancifully christened Doctor Jekyll. She didn't know how
deep her feelings went, she would only know that when
she saw him again with her eyes free of the blinkers of the
past. She only knew for now that she didn't want to lose
that man, that her life would be poorer if she never saw
him again.

'I want to find Cal, to tell him all this—all that I've
discovered about myself—and see if we can start again.'
Her breath caught in her throat as she turned to Ricky,
clasping his hand tightly. 'I *have* to see him again!' she
cried, her grey eyes lighting with conviction.

Ricky's smile was gentle 'At last you're thinking of

what *you* want,' he said with a laugh. 'So what's stopping you?'

The light faded from Helen's eyes, leaving them dark and dull as a November sky.

'I don't know where to find him, Ricky. I don't even know where he lives, except on a farm somewhere in Yorkshire.'

Her brother's smile widened into a grin and he carefully eased his hand from her clinging grasp.

'If that's the only problem,' he said getting to his feet, 'then I think I have the answer.'

He crossed the room to the desk that stood in the corner, taking the envelope with his name on it from its polished surface and pulling out the cheque as he came back to stand beside her.

'This place,' he said, pointing to the name of the branch of the bank printed on the slip of paper,' is a very small Yorkshire village. I doubt if there are more than a few hundred inhabitants in all. If you go there, I reckon it should be quite an easy job to find one particular farmer named Calder Hyde.'

CHAPTER EIGHT

'IT should be quite an easy job to find one particular farmer named Calder Hyde.'

Ricky's words echoed in Helen's head as she got out of her car and walked to lean on the dry stone wall, staring out at the farm buildings spread before her. She had never expected it to be quite so easy, but now she saw the size of Cal's home she wasn't surprised that the first person she had approached as she entered Roscombe village had responded so quickly.

'Calder Hyde's place?' he said in his soft Yorkshire accent. 'Oh, yes, I know where that is. Just follow this road straight through the village and then keep on it for another couple of miles. You can't miss it.'

And for once those often mistakenly used words 'You can't miss it' had been accurate. No one could have missed the spread of buildings with the farmhouse itself set slightly back from them, its pale stonework glowing in the mellow light of the afternoon sun.

Just how much of this land did he actually own? she wondered, surveying the patchwork of green and gold fields before her. There wasn't another farmhouse to be seen for miles. When Cal had spoken of his father's farm, she had imagined a small, comfortable home, not this—but then, remembering the amount Cal had paid in ransom, she supposed she should have been prepared for something bigger than her rather naïve imaginings.

That thought brought a frown to her face, her grey eyes clouding as a faint breeze flicked the long strands of her

silky black hair forward and over her face. She pushed it
back with a despondent sigh. It had all seemed so easy
last night when, fired by Ricky's enthusiasm, she had
determined on this expedition to Yorkshire.

There had been no problem getting the necessary time
off work. She had her full year's quota of leave still owing
to her, not having taken a holiday since those ill-fated
days that should have been her honeymoon, and it had
been a simple matter to persuade Mr Crown to let her
have one or two days off even at such short notice, so that
her spirits had been high as Ricky waved her off.

'Go for it, Sis!' he had declared enthusiastically. 'You
have to fight for what you want.'

Fight. Helen could have wished he had chosen some
other word. Now that she was actually here, the prospect
of meeting Cal loomed on the horizon like a dark rain-
cloud. Just how would he react when she turned up
literally on his doorstep after telling him that she never
wanted to see him again? She could hardly expect that he
would be pleased to see her. She had driven all this way
simply to see Cal, in the hope of being able to talk to him,
to explain, to tell him everything that, with Ricky's help,
she had found out about herself, but she could only do
that if he gave her the chance. After the things she had
said, could she really expect him to give her that chance?
He was far more likely to simply slam the door shut in her
face.

But having come this far, could she turn round and go
back now without ever having seen him? Helen had
barely had time even to ask herself the question before
she knew the answer had to be no. She could not turn
back now. Whatever happened she had to go through
with this.

The sound of the doorbell pealing through the hall in

the large old farmhouse set Helen's nerves jangling in response. Footsteps sounded on the tiled floor and Helen's heart stopped dead as she saw the tall, masculine figure, golden hair gleaming in the sunlight, approaching through the glass panes in the door. Her hands tightened convulsively on her bag and the racing of her pulse was like the roar of thunder in her ears. Her mouth was painfully dry, her throat aching with stress so that she felt she would never be able to speak. Then the door opened and she found herself staring straight into the vivid green eyes she so longed for and yet dreaded to see, steeling herself for the moment when they changed, hardening against her.

Surprisingly, the change didn't come. Instead she saw only a swift flash of appreciation followed by a mild and smiling curiosity before the man said, 'Yes? Can I help you?'

It was his voice that jolted her into thought. Deep and very slightly husky, it was an attractive voice, but not the one she had been expecting to hear. As the haze of shock faded from her mind, she managed to focus more clearly on the man before her, taking in his appearance fully for the first time. Cal—and yet not Cal. She couldn't have defined the difference in specific terms, but every instinct told her it was there, and the sight of the tiny delicate butterfly tattooed at the base of the man's throat only confirmed what she had known intuitively already.

'You must be Joel!' She blurted out the words without thinking, only realising that if Joel was here, at the farm, he wouldn't want his identity known when she saw the touch of suspicion that darkened those vivid green eyes. 'I've come to see Cal,' she put in hurriedly. 'I'm not a reporter.'

'No, you're not.' Joel Hyde's smile came easily, that

hint of suspicion vanishing as swiftly as it had come.

'How—how did you know?' Helen stammered in confusion. Having nerved herself for a meeting with Cal, only to find his brother instead, she now felt the effects of reaction set in. They were so alike! she thought dazedly. It was no wonder no one at the party had ever guessed.

'You know about Cal,' he pointed out. 'And you said Joel. Most people who don't know my brother call me Jay.'

She hadn't thought of that. In fact she had actually forgotten about Jay Keller's existence. Even before Cal had revealed the truth about his identity she had almost ceased to think of him as Jay Keller, the rock star, seeing him only as Cal Hyde, the man to whom she was becoming more attracted with every minute that passed.

And now she was confronted by the real Jay Keller, the man they should have kidnapped if by that strange twist of fate Cal had not taken his place. How would she have felt then? Joel had the same eyes, the same mane of golden hair, though without the threads of copper that laced his brother's. They had the same clean-cut features and firmly compact body—so why, after that first lurching shock of panic at thinking he was Cal, wasn't her heart racing with the excitement that Cal seemed to be able to induce simply by existing? The two brothers were definitely identical, almost frighteningly alike, so how was it possible that one could throw her mentally off balance while the other, Joel, simply inspired an objective appreciation of a singularly attractive specimen of the male sex?

Suddenly Helen became aware of the way she was staring and a hot wave of embarrassment swept over her.

'I—I'm sorry——'

But Joel smiled at her discomfiture.

'We have that effect on most people,' he told her laughingly. 'Don't worry, I'm quite used to it.' And he was, Helen realised. He was used not only to the shocked reaction from someone realising how alike he and his brother were, but also to having people stare at him in this way. This was Jay Keller, the showman, the man who had thousands of fans screaming for him—not Cal. 'Cal's out at the moment,' Joel went on. 'But he'll be back for lunch. Perhaps you'd like to come in and wait.'

For a second Helen knew a cowardly impulse to say no, she would leave it, come back another time, but then she got a grip on her fast-draining courage. The sight of Joel had rocked her sense of reality, but she couldn't back down now. If she gave in to her craven impulse she would never find the nerve to come back again.

'If you don't mind. I wouldn't be disturbing you?'

'Not at all,' was the light-hearted answer. 'As a matter of fact, I'd be glad of some company. I came up here for a break after recording but, quite frankly, all this rural peace and quiet is beginning to pall.'

And there was another difference between the brothers, Helen reflected as she followed him across the hall. Cal had spoken of the farm with love, he would never find its peace and quiet boring and, personally, she felt that she never would either. It seemed like a haven from the rush and bustle of town life. Joel led her into a warm, sun-filled sitting-room and, glancing round, Helen could not suppress an exclamation of delight.

'What a lovely room!' she declared spontaneously, taking in the cream-painted walls speckled with sunlight and the shadows of a huge ivy growing up the wall outside, the rich golds and browns of the traditionally styled settee and chairs, their colours echoed in the thick velvet curtains hanging at the windows. None of the furnishings were new, the soft cushions on the armchairs were slightly worn, but the whole room had a comfortable, lived-in air. It was a family room, the heart of a home.

'Do you like it?' Joel asked. 'I prefer something more modern myself, but Cal likes it this way. Can I get you some coffee or something?'

'Coffee would be lovely,' Helen told him gratefully, appreciating the thought of a few moments to herself as much as the idea of a drink after her long drive.

'Coming up! I won't be a minute.'

Joel disappeared in search of the drinks and, left alone, Helen wandered around the room, just looking, touching an ornament here or there, trying to clear her mind, calm herself, so that she could think what she would say when she finally met Cal face to face. Really she had no idea what explanation she was going to give him for appearing at his home like this.

It was much warmer inside, the mild spring sunshine concentrated through the large windows that gave such a wonderful view of carefully tended gardens, and Helen slipped out of her jacket, laying it carefully on the back of one of the big armchairs, a small smile curving her lips at the memory of how she had agonised over what to wear on this trip. She had been tempted by the thought of her denim jeans, recalling Cal's enthusiastic and frankly sensual reaction to them during the time he had been in her house, but in the end had decided against them and in favour of a white knitted cotton suit with a V-necked top and a pencil skirt that clung to her slim hips and showed off her long legs, its colour a perfect foil for the gleaming blue-black of her hair.

'I told the housekeeper you'd be staying to lunch.' Joel had reappreared with a tray of coffee-things. 'And no,' he added swiftly to forestall the protest she had obviously been about to make, 'it's no trouble. Any friend of Cal's is welcome any time.'

Friend. The word stabbed like a cold knife. Helen doubted very much if Cal would ever describe her as a friend. Not for the first time she wondered if she had been very foolish even to think of coming here.

'Have you known Cal long?' Joel's polite enquiry jolted her out of her troublesome thoughts.

'No—not long. As a matter of fact I only met him last week.'

'Last week!' Joel turned a startled face towards her. 'But—good lord, don't tell me *you're* the terrorist who kidnapped him.'

Helen almost choked on her coffee. 'He told you!' she managed in a hoarse, uneven gasp.

Joel nodded, a grin stretching his lips wide and his eyes sparkling jewel-bright with delighted laughter.

'He told me,' he confirmed. 'I suppose in a way it's largely my fault—I got him into it when I asked him to take my place so I could get away quickly. It should have been me you kidnapped, so the least I could do was pay half of the "ransom".' He flashed Helen a swift, blatantly flirtatious smile. 'I wish I'd never asked Cal to stand in for me now. If I'd known *you* were to be my kidnapper I'd have gone very quietly, I can assure you.'

That smile was infectious and Helen felt her own lips curving in response to it. On the surface at least, Joel was much easier to get on with than his brother, his light-hearted flirting so different from the prickly, hostile man Cal had been on the first day in her house—which made it all the more strange that that was *all* she felt. Her expression sobered rapidly on that thought. What was it about Cal that made the difference?

'But tell me,' Joel was saying, 'what did you do to Cal while he was with you? He's not been himself at all since he came back. He only gave me the briefest of outlines of what had happened, and when I wanted to know more he almost bit my head off and, believe me, that's not at all like him. So what happened between you?'

The brief lightening of Helen's spirits vanished swiftly at his words. Joel's description of Cal's mood was hardly encouraging in view of the prospect of the coming meeting. She had opened her mouth to speak—though what she would say she had no idea—but any words died in her throat, for at that moment the door was pushed open and Cal himself strode into the room.

'Joel, I——' He broke off abruptly, his eyes going straight to Helen's white face. 'You!'

Not the most auspicious of beginnings, Helen thought on a wave of panic, all the carefully thought-out opening lines she had rehearsed over and over in the car during her journey to Yorkshire fading from her mind, driven away by the shock of seeing him now, when she was so completely unprepared.

But in the next second the shock had receded and all she could think of was the sense of pure delight that simply seeing Cal brought, setting her pulse racing so that her heart seemed to be beating high up in her throat. After her mild response to Joel, so physically like his brother, she had begun to wonder if she had exaggerated the way Cal could make her feel, but now she knew that, if anything, she had underestimated badly, pushing to the back of her mind the sheer physical impact of his forceful masculinity. Even now, dressed in a faded shirt and well-worn denim jeans, clothes so very different from the elegant suit in which she had first seen him, just the sight of him had the effect of a physical blow in her stomach, driving all the breath from her body so that she could only sit as if frozen in her seat, incapable of managing a single word of response.

'What are you doing here?' Cal demanded, his voice hard and cold.

Helen could find no words to answer him and it was Joel, plainly disconcerted by his brother's reaction, who broke the strained silence that followed Cal's angry question.

'She came to see you.' He turned to Helen, an apologetic smile of his face. 'I'm sorry, I didn't ask your name.'

'It's Helen, Helen Seymour.' Cal supplied the answer and Helen felt she had never heard her name spoken with such distaste, the words coming out clipped and curt, no trace of warmth lightening the harshness of Cal's tone. 'This, Joel, is the young lady——' Helen flinched at the scathing note that turned that 'lady' into a searing insult '—who wanted to kidnap you, but got me instead.'

'I know, she's already admitted to her crimes.'

Joel was clearly trying to make a joke in order to lighten the atmosphere, but his efforts fell on very stony ground, no hint of a response showing on Cal's face. It might have been carved out of stone, Helen thought miserably, it was so set and hard.

If she had the strength, if her legs would only carry her, she would get up and run. Coming here had been a terrible mistake. Cal would never forgive the things she had said, one swift glance at his face had told her that only too clearly.

'If you don't mind, Joel,' Cal addressed his brother, 'I'd like to speak to Miss Seymour alone.'

'OK,' Joel agreed easily, getting to his feet. 'I'll see you later, Helen—I invited her for lunch,' he added in response to his brother's questioning frown, a frown that darkened swiftly at his reply, showing exactly how Cal felt about the invitation.

Helen wished she could find something to say, anything that would keep Joel in the room with them so that she didn't have to face Cal on her own because now that the moment had come she knew she couldn't handle it, would never find the right words to say. But Joel was already heading out of the door and her voice seemed to have deserted her completely so that she couldn't have called him back even if she had tried.

'So what the hell are you doing here?'

Helen could have sworn it was impossible for Cal to inject any more coldness into his voice, but the tone in which the question was flung at her chilled her through to the bone, turning her blood to ice in her veins.

'Well?' Cal demanded when she didn't answer.

At last Helen found the strength to speak. 'I wanted to—talk to you.'

'Talk!' Cal's laugh was harsh and totally without humour, a cruel, frightening sound that Helen flinched away from instinctively. 'Lady, you and I are well past the point of talking. I have nothing to say to you and you've said everything I ever want to hear.'

'But——' In desperation Helen seized on the first idea that came into her mind. 'But I wanted to thank you.'

'For what?'

'For the——' She found the word hard to say. 'The ransom. There was no need for you to have paid it at all, I never expected you to. It was very generous of you.'

'Generous!' Cal echoed the word sardonically. 'It wasn't generous at all. That ransom as you call it was supposed to have been the price of my freedom. I wanted to make damn sure that you didn't come after me, looking for a contribution to your precious appeal funds.'

'But I wouldn't have done that!' Helen was unable to hide the pain in her voice. She should have expected this, she told herself despondently, should have expected that every trace of Doctor Jekyll would be hidden under the mask of Mr Hyde, but it still hurt so badly, Cal's bitterness stabbing her to the heart.

'No, I don't suppose you would.' To her intense relief some of the attacking quality had left Cal's voice. 'That was unfair of me. I apologise. I wanted to contribute. As I said, I think it's a very worthwhile cause.

'And I wanted to thank you.' Could she allow herself to believe that those words, stiff and formally polite as they had been, meant that he was actually beginning to soften? Cal's next statement killed that fragile hope before it was fully born.

'Joel paid his share,' he said dismissively. 'It was a joint donation.'

'I know, he told me.'

'And did you thank him, too?' Cal's tone was searingly sarcastic. 'Well, now you've done everything you came for perhaps you'll get in your car and go. I don't want you here, Helen.'

'But, Cal——' Helen began then stopped, not knowing how to go on. How could she fight that adamant 'I don't want you here'? There was so much she wanted to tell him, so much she wanted to explain, but she didn't know where to begin. How could she express all that she had discovered about herself when she wasn't even sure that Cal would listen?

'But Cal, nothing!' Cal declared harshly. 'I want you to go—just get out and leave me in peace!'

It was the last few words that gave him away, a tiny chink in the armour of coldness that surrounded him.

There had been a raw edge to his voice when he had spoken them, one that spoke of a pain he had tried to bury deep inside himself and had not quite succeeded. She had hurt him badly with her unthinking words, hurt him far more than she had ever realised, and her conscience stung cruelly at the thought, making it even more important that she did explain—if only she could get through to him, make him listen.

'Cal, please——' she tried again, but at that moment the door swung open.

'Lunch is ready,' Joel announced, totally oblivious of his appalling timing.

Under any other circumstances, Helen felt she would have thoroughly enjoyed having lunch at Valley Farm. The food was delicious and Joel had clearly set himself to being charming, drawing her out with interested questions and adding his own brand of sparkling wit that had her laughing uninhibitedly.

But all the time she was supremely conscious of the broodingly silent figure of Cal sitting opposite her, his presence as ominous as a black thundercloud at a summer picnic. She knew he was listening to every word she said and that made it all the more difficult to respond naturally and spontaneously, particularly when Joel teased her about the kidnapping.

'You know what they say about kidnappers and their victims,' he said lightly with a sly glance at his brother's unresponsive face. 'It's a well known fact that they often fall madly in love with each other.'

Helen's knife landed on her plate with a clatter and her eyes flew to Cal's face, meeting a relentlessly stony look from his emerald eyes.

'In this case that theory doesn't apply,' he said with a complete lack of any emotion at all. 'The relationship between Helen and myself was strictly a business one.'

'Oh, come on!' Joel laughed. 'Are you trying to say that you spent four days alone in a house with a beautiful woman and——'

'I'm not *trying* to say anything,' Cal cut in sharply. 'I'm simply stating a fact.'

Stating it for whose benefit? Helen wondered miserably. That look had told her that his words were directed as much at her as at his brother. Oh, she had been crazy to come here, crazy to hope that they could ever start again. Cal had built up a wall between them, a wall so strong and solid that she doubted if she had the strength ever to break it down—and yet there had been that revealing 'Leave me in peace'. Would she be a fool to pin her hopes on that? And would Cal ever let her get close enough to find out?

Cal pushed his chair back. 'I have to get back to work.'

'Why don't you take the afternoon off and show Helen around the farm?' Joel suggested. 'After all, she's driven a long way to see you. Would you like that, Helen?'

I'd love it! The words formed on Helen's lips, inspired by the hope that if she and Cal had some time by themselves she might just find the right moment to speak to him, but the thought died unspoken when she looked at Cal's unyielding face, hastily amended to, 'If Cal has the time.'

'I've too much to do this afternoon.' Cal's tone gave away as little as his face.

'Then I'll do the honours,' Joel put in. 'If you'll accept me as an escort, Helen.'

'Of course.'

Too late Helen saw the muscle that moved in Cal's cheek, indicating a sudden tension. 'I never wanted you,' she'd said. 'I thought you were Jay Keller.' And now here was the real Jay Keller offering to be her escort and she could just imagine exactly how Cal had interpreted her acceptance. She felt as if she was spinning wildly on a merry-go-round that was out of control and she couldn't get off. It's not what you think! she wanted to cry. It's not like that at all! But the words wouldn't come and Cal had left the room before the whirling in her head slowed and eased.

It was a glorious afternoon, warm with sunshine and with the scent of grass and flowers on the air, and Joel was the most flatteringly attentive escort any woman could have wanted as he took her round the farm buildings and out into the fields. His conversation was light and undemanding, his wit as bright and sparkling as it had been at lunch, so that Helen found herself relaxing, enjoying herself in spite of the persistent worry that nagged at her mind, the fretting question whether she would ever be able to talk to Cal on her own and if he would listen to her—or would she have to leave at the end of the day with nothing resolved, knowing that the distance was still there between them and was likely to remain there for ever?

'Didn't you ever want to stay here yourself?' she asked Joel as they leaned against a fence watching a flock of ewes with their lambs who delighted Helen with their carefree behaviour, chasing after each other on delicate hooves, small tails flicking in the air.

'Lord, no!' was Joel's response. 'The farm's all right to retreat to when I need a rest after a tour, but I could never live here. I find the quiet gets to me after a while. I'm a big-city man myself, I like the bright lights, the noise, the activity. I could never settle here, I'd be bored out of my skull, wouldn't you?'

'No.'

Helen's answer came slowly, her eyes still on the lambs. Standing here like this with the warmth of the sun on her back and the song of the birds in her ears she felt strangely as if she had come home. She had had to move to the city because of her job, but she had carefully chosen her home as far out in the suburbs as possible in order to be away from the bustle and traffic of the city centre.

'No,' she said more firmly. 'I could stay here for ever.'

'We'll have to agree to differ, then,' Joel told her cheerfully, his grin as infectious as before, bringing a smile to Helen's lips too.

The more time she spent with Joel, the more she could imagine this brother as Jay Keller, the man she had described as the showman. His light-hearted, casual flirting fitted much more with the stage act she had seen, an act she now found it impossible to believe she had ever considered Cal could have taken part in. Unhappily she recalled Cal's own comments on the show when she had first met him. If only she had listened to him properly instead of being blinded by her own prejudices she might have realised then that he was not the man she took him to be. A faint sigh escaped her lips. If only she hadn't stopped Cal when he had tried to explain, then perhaps things might have been so very different. But she *had* stopped him and now this yawning chasm gaped between them, one she did not know how to bridge.

'Do you have to go back tonight?' Joel's voice interrupted her unhappy thoughts, jolting her back into the present.

'I—well, no I don't, not really.'

Her words came as a surprise, even to herself. When she had rung the office that morning she had said she wasn't quite sure when she would be back, tomorrow or the day after, and Mr Crown had told her to take as long as she needed. She could easily take another day off if she wanted—but did she want to?

The answer came with a stunning speed. She had no desire at all to return home and bury herself in her work as she had done after David's desertion. Ricky had said that she didn't think enough of what *she* wanted and perhaps he was right, but she knew what she wanted now. It didn't matter if it was irrational, illogical, even irresponsible, she *wanted* to stay here, wanted it with all her heart.

'No,' she said definitely, her mind made up. 'I don't have to go back tonight.'

'Then would you like to stay here?' Joel asked. 'It can be arranged quite easily.'

If she stayed she would have another night and most of tomorrow, hours more in Cal's company, many more chances to get closer to him and try to explain.

'I'd love to.' Helen's heart soared briefly at the prospect, then plummeted as swiftly with the memory of Cal's reaction when he had first seen her.

'But—would Cal mind?' she asked awkwardly. 'It is his house, after all—he might not want——'

'Oh, leave Cal to me.' Joel dismissed her stumbling protests with an airy wave.' He's always said the farm's still my home, even though I don't own any of it any more. If I say I've invited you he'll raise no objections.'

'If you say so.' Helen wished she could have Joel's confidence.

'Just leave it to me.' Joel flashed her a brilliant smile, then abruptly his expression sobered. 'Helen, I hope you don't think I'm prying, but what happened between you and Cal?'

'What happened?' The question had caught Helen totally unprepared and she could think of no way to answer him. 'Nothing,' she managed at last, her voice low and unsure. 'What makes you think there is anything between us at all?'

'Instinct perhaps,' Joel laughed. 'Cal's my brother— my twin. If anyone knows how his mind works it has to be me and I know he's not been himself ever since he got back—since he left you. Oh, he has his moods, but this one's different. He's been going round with a face as black as a thundercloud and he's as irritable as hell. I'm not blind, either. I saw his face when he saw you, he looked like a man who'd seen a ghost come back to haunt him.'

'Joel, please!' Helen broke in hastily, unable to take any more. 'Please believe me when I tell you that there is *nothing* between us.' The words caught in her throat as her heart cried out against the realisation that they were closer to the truth than she dared admit. 'Nothing at all. We—I——'

Taking a deep breath, she decided that it was best to stick to the story she had told Cal himself.

'He left in quite a rush—before I'd seen the cheque he'd left. I wanted to thank him personally.'

Well, at least that was half the truth, if nowhere near all of it, she told herself miserably, and something twisted deep in her heart at the thought of how much she had left out, the things that still remained hidden.

'There's nothing else,' she repeated rather desperately.

'OK, if you say so.' Joel did not sound as if he fully believed her and Helen could only pray that he was more convinced than he seemed. If not, he might challenge Cal on the same subject to see if their stories tallied. Helen's blood turned cold at the thought and she found herself reconsidering her earlier enthusiastic response to Joel's suggestion that she stayed overnight.

'Perhaps I'd better not——' she began but, clearly anticipating what she had been about to say, Joel forestalled her.

'You can't change your mind now,' he told her. 'It's all settled. You're staying. In fact we'll go and tackle Cal about it now.'

'Joel——' Helen tried to protest, but he was already moving away, heading towards the farm buildings where they had seen Cal a few minutes before.

It was cool and dark inside the barn in strong contrast to the brightneess of the sunlight outside, and for a few moments Helen blinked uncertainly, trying to adjust her eyes to the change in the light. Dimly she saw Cal's strong figure, recognisable only because of the brightness of his hair, and with a fluttering nervous sensation in her stomach heard Joel's voice explaining the proposed plan. As he finished speaking her eyes cleared and immediately she wished they hadn't as she caught the coldly assesing glance Cal slanted at her face, his green eyes narrowing thoughtfully.

'And would you like to stay, Miss Seymour?' he asked and, shocked by the thinly veiled hostility in that icy tone, Helen could only nod silently.

For a long minute Cal didn't speak, apparently considering his decision, and in that moment Helen felt all her muscles tighten, drawing taut with tension until they ached as Cal's silence gave her unwanted time to have second and then third thoughts about her decision to stay.

'The farm's your home as much as mine, Joel.'

And that was that. A few seconds later he had turned away, returning to his work without apparently giving them a second thought. Seeing Joel's triumphant grin, Helen knew that he interpreted those few brusque words as an acceptance, but she herself could not be so sure. What had been hidden behind those hooded, shuttered eyes? She couldn't begin to guess at the thoughts Cal was so carefully concealing, but as she watched him walk away, the stiff way he held his shoulders and his head betraying an inner tension that matched her own, her heart twisted in despair. How was she ever going to explain if he never let her close enough even to talk to him? She was determined to have one more try but, not knowing exactly what his mood might be, she was going to have to use all her instincts when she saw Cal again.

In the event she saw little of him at all that evening. He did not appear for dinner, having sent a message to say that one of the cows had started to calve and as she was having some difficulty he had decided to stay with her. There was no way of judging the truth of this statement, short of going out to the cowsheds to see for herself, and Helen was left to wonder if she was being unduly sensitive or had Cal's story simply been an excuse, a reason to avoid seeing her any more than he actually had to? She couldn't know, but the suspicion burned in her thoughts like a searing white-hot knife, making her wish that she had never stayed, that she was anywhere but here.

But she had accepted the invitation, a bed had been made up for her and it would be churlish to change her mind now. A hard, painful knot formed in the pit of Helen's stomach at the memory of Ricky's delight when she had telephoned him to explain that she would not be back that night. He had immediately assumed that this was because things were going well, that she and Cal had come to some understanding, and she had had a hard time explaining that this was not in fact the case.

'It isn't what you think, Ricky,' she had protested

weakly, but her brother had laughed off her doubts.

'You're there, aren't you—and he hasn't sent you packing. That's a start, Nell. What you make of it is up to you.'

'But Ricky——' Helen's words went unheard.

'Keep fighting, Sis,' her brother declared. 'Make sure that this time you get what you really want.'

Helen had replaced the receiver slowly, a frown creasing her forehead as she leaned back against the wall in the darkened hallway. 'Make sure you get what you really want'—but what *did* she want? She had come here because she had wanted to see Cal one more time and because she had wanted to explain her actions to him in the light of everything Ricky had taught her about herself. And now she had seen Cal, but as for explaining—well, there she was as far away from achieving that desire as ever, if not further than when she had set off. In fact, coming here had just been a waste of time. Nothing had changed.

Or had it? Wearily Helen rubbed a hand across her forehead. Something had changed—in her, at least. The half-formed resolves that had sent her out to Valley Farm in the first place had now reshaped and hardened into something very different. The time she had spent walking round the farm with Joel had taught her that she wanted more than just to see Cal and explain. If that had been the case, she could have enjoyed Joel's company without that nagging sense of loss and incompleteness.

To be with a man so like Cal that they were almost impossible to tell apart, and yet feel only dissatisfaction and an aching longing could mean only one thing. She wanted *Cal* and only him, and wanted him in a way that went deeper than the desire she had felt for him on the night he had made love to her. But how deep did that feeling go? Helen sighed. That was something she had no way of knowing.

Cal had not returned to the house by the time dusk fell, as Helen and Joel sat together in the comfortable living-room. In spite of the warmth of the day, the evening had brought a chill to the atmosphere, necessitating the lighting of a fire in the open grate, and they had left the curtains undrawn and the lights off, sitting in the glow of the coals as they chatted.

'Does Cal often work this late?' Helen said, hiding the questions she really wanted to ask, the need to know if Cal was avoiding her, behind a casual enquiry.

'Spring and summer's often like this,' was Joel's response. 'There are farmhands who can do the job just as well, of course, but Cal's a perfectionist. He likes to be involved, he really cares about those beasts of his.'

'Yes.' She got to her feet restlessly, moving away from the fire and into the shadows to hide the betraying rosiness of her cheeks. 'Don't you think someone should take him something to eat—some coffee, at least?'

'He'll come in when he's ready.' Joel stretched lazily and in the half-light of the fire his face was suddenly so like Cal's that Helen's breath caught painfully in her throat, almost choking her. 'What's up, Helen? You're like a cat on hot bricks.'

'I don't know—I just felt restless.'

It was no explanation and she knew it, and from the frown that crossed his face Joel knew it, too.

'Come and sit down.' He patted the cushions on the settee at his side. 'That's better,' he smiled as she took up the position he had indicated. 'Now, what's troubling you?'

You are! Helen wanted to cry. Because you're so like Cal, and yet you're not him. If Cal's looks had been all

that had attracted her, then to be with Joel should not
have made any difference, but somehow it made all the
difference in the world and the possible repercussions of
that thought made her shiver in spite of the heat from the
fire. Immediately she felt Joel's arm come round her
shoulders.

'What is it?' he asked softly, but Helen could only
shake her head, incapable of answering him for fear he
would hear the unhappiness in her voice. She kept her
head bent so that he would not see the glimmer of tears in
her eyes, and so she did not see the shadow of a man that
darkened the uncurtained window for a moment and
then moved away.

'Helen?'

Joel's voice was soothing, his arm around her warm
and comforting, the shoulder against which she buried
her face strong and dependable, but in her misery Helen
was only too aware that his were not the arms she needed
or the voice she wanted to hear. A sob choked in her
throat and she was unable to suppress it.

'Helen!' Joel said on a note of shocked concern.

With gentle fingers he turned her face to his so that she
was forced to meet his eyes, seeing how they caught the
sparks of the firelight. Pain stabbed deep into Helen's
heart at the thought that it had been a pair of clear bright
eyes, so like Joel's, that had first attracted her.

'Is there anything I can do?' Joel asked and once more
she shook her head, not trusting her voice to speak.

Joel's head bent towards her. He was going to kiss her,
Helen realised dazedly—and she was going to let him.
Because only then would she know, only then would she
be sure.

Joel's lips were warm and firm, his kiss gentle, and

Helen accepted it without restraint or hesitation, and suddenly there was no uncertainty any more, only the blinding white light of realisation that left her breathless and dizzy, her head reeling as if from a blow. Joel was his brother's double and yet his kiss meant nothing other than a gesture of affection. It awoke no longings in her, aroused no painfully aching yearning for more. In a second of heart-stopping revelation she knew without any shadow of a doubt and once and for all exactly what she felt. She *loved* Cal, she didn't know how or when it had happened, but none of that mattered. All that was important was the knowledge that she loved Cal Hyde with every ounce of feeling of which she was capable.

'Joel——' she breathed unsteadily. 'Joel—I——'

She got no further for at that moment the light was switched on with a shattering abruptness, flooding the room with light so that Helen blinked furiously, temporarily blinded, the strong figure in the doorway only a vague and indistinct blur.

'I beg your pardon, Joel,' Cal's voice was harsh and bitterly sardonic. 'I didn't realise I was interrupting anything.'

CHAPTER NINE

'CAL!'

Helen's cry was a sound of shock, despair and pleading all rolled into one. How long had Cal been there? How much had he seen? She wanted to tell him he had got it all wrong, that it hadn't been as it had seemed, but the words died on her lips as she saw the flash of cold anger in his burning green eyes, the tautness of the muscles around his mouth and jaw etching white marks of controlled fury on to his face.

Joel, however, appeared completely unperturbed by his brother's sudden appearnace and dangerous expression.

'You're not interrupting anything,' he said easily. 'Come in and sit down, you must be worn out. How's the prize heifer?'

'She'll do.'

Cal moved to sit in one of the armchairs, leaning back in his seat and rubbing his hand across his eyes in a gesture of weariness. He looked drained and tired, the shirt and jeans he wore crumpled and stained, but in Helen's eyes he had never seemed more devastatingly attractive. Having admitted that she loved him, it was as if she was seeing him through new eyes, so that she wondered how she could ever have thought that he and Joel were even remotely alike. He was the only man she wanted and her heart clenched painfully at the knowledge of his physical closeness when the gaping chasm still stretched between them mentally.

'Have you had anything to eat?'

Joel's casual question, his conversational tone sounded alien to Helen in her hypersensitive state. It seemed impossible that neither of the two men in the room could hear the pounding of her heart that sounded like the roar of thunder in her ears.

'No time,' was Cal's abrupt reply.

'Perhaps I could get you something.' Helen found her voice at last, drawing that clear-eyed gaze to her face once more.

Immediately she wished she hadn't spoken. The scathing contempt that burned in Cal's eyes seemed to scorch her skin, making her painfully aware of the fact that Joel's arm still rested about her shoulders so that she made an uneasy little move away from him. Joel made no attempt to resist her, but let his arm slide down on to the back of the settee.

'That's an idea,' he said. 'I could do with a cup of coffee myself, couldn't you, Cal?'

His brother's only response was a curt nod, but Helen seized thankfully on the excuse to leave the room. She needed time to get a grip on herself, regain some composure.

In the kitchen she leaned weakly against the wall, struggling to control the trembling that shook her body in reaction to the shock of Cal's sudden arrival. How long had he been standing unseen in the doorway watching them? Her heart ached at the thought of just what interpretation Cal would put on the scene he had interrupted. She had come here to try to get close to him, but instead it seemed that she had driven him even further away than ever, and it was the bitterest irony that this should have happened so soon after she had come to realise exactly how she felt about him.

It was some minutes before she was controlled enough to make the coffee. Finding bread and some cold roast beef, she made several sandwiches, too. Cal had had nothing to eat since lunch time, he would need some food. In spite of her troubled feelings, Helen found a whole new pleasure in the simple task of slicing and buttering bread, knowing that she was doing this small thing for the man she loved. But that pleasure was mixed with a deep despair at the fear that Cal might never know of her love, or if he did he might not believe in it.

It came as a distinct shock when she returned to the living-room to discover that there was only one tall, fair-haired figure in the room and Joel had disappeared.

'Joel's gone to bed,' Cal told her emotionlessly, his keen green eyes missing nothing of her loss of colour and the anxious glance she cast around the room. 'He decided to dispense with the coffee.'

Whose idea had that been? Helen wondered frantically. Had Joel really decided to go, or had his brother been responsible for his unexpected departure?

'I suggested he went, actually,' Cal added, picking up her thoughts with uncanny sensitivity so that she could almost believe he had read her mind, not too difficult a job as her thoughts were written all too clearly on her face. 'I thought it was time we had a talk.'

'Talk!' Helen echoed hollowly, unable to believe what she was hearing.

'Oh, come on, Helen,' Cal taunted. 'You said that was what you wanted when you came here—don't tell me you're going to chicken out now.'

'You said there was nothing to talk about.' Helen's

voice sounded stiff and tight, hiding her true feelings behind a mask of pride. How could she talk to him now, when his antagonism radiated from him like heat from the fire? Her hands shook so that the cups on the tray she was carrying rattled against each other, betraying the nervous movement, and with an abrupt, jerky gesture she set the tray down on the table, wanting to hide her weakness. 'I think I'll go to bed too,' she said in a low, despondent voice.

She was half-way to the door when Cal's hand fastened around her wrist in a bruising grip, jerking her to a halt with such force that she swung round involuntarily, coming face to face with him. Her heart quailed inside her at the sight of the marks of anger and tension on his face, drawing every muscle tight over his strong bones. Yellow flames of fury flared in the green eyes making her shiver convulsively.

'Please let me go, Cal,' she pleaded unhappily.

'No.' Cal shook his head adamantly. 'There are things I have to know.'

With an effort Helen drew on her fast-dwindling reserves of strength and from deep inside her found the courage to meet those burning eyes, her own grey ones clouded and dull with misery.

'What sort of things, Cal?' She had a better control over her voice now and it barely shook on the words. 'What is there to find out? You've made your position crystal clear.'

'And so have you.' Cal's voice was a low, savage snarl. 'But I never thought you'd take things this far. Tell me— are you satisfied?'

'Satisfied?' Helen wished she didn't keep repeating his words like a dazed parrot, but her mind felt so bruised she was incapable of rational thought. 'I don't know what you mean.'

'"I don't know what you mean",' Cal's echoing of her statement didn't sound dazed at all, it was an expression of pure scorn. There was no sign of Doctor Jekyll now, he was pure Hyde through and through. 'Oh, lady, do you expect me to believe that?' "I don't want you",' he quoted so viciously that Helen flinched at the bitterness he injected into her own thoughtless words. '"I thought you were Jay Keller"—and when you found I wasn't you weren't satisfied—you sent me away. But you couldn't leave things alone, you came here, looking for Joel, and now you've found him, you've got what you wanted.' Cal's voice rose to a shout. 'I want to know if you're bloody well satisfied!'

'No.' Helen's head moved in an instinctive denial of his words, her voice low and despairing. 'No, Cal, I——'

'No?' he cut in sneeringly. 'So you're not satisfied—and why is that, I wonder? Did I interrupt things too soon, my lovely Helen? Did you plan to get my brother into your bed, too? Is that what you wanted?'

'No!' It came out high and sharp. She couldn't tell if he was hiding pain behind anger, couldn't tell if there was anything she could reach behind the cruel, cold mask that was his face, she only knew she had to stop him talking like this. 'It wasn't like that at all!'

'Then what was it like?' Cal's bitter tongue lashed her mercilessly. 'How did you feel when you got what you wanted—when you were in my brother's arms? Did it excite you, Helen? Did it give you what you needed?'

Helen wanted to scream another denial, wanted to lift her hand to wipe that taunting look from Cal's face, but even as her lips moved to form the words she saw the swift and suddenly shocking change that came over Cal's expression. His eyes darkened until they seemed almost black as with a forceful and irresistible pressure on her arm he drew her inexorably closer.

'Did you enjoy Joel's kisses, my lovely?' he asked, his voice strangely rough and husky. 'Did they give you what you wanted?'

Mesmerised by this new and inexplicable mood, Helen couldn't struggle, but let him pull her close against him so that her slender body was pressed tight against the firm hard length of his.

'Did he kiss you like this, Helen?' Cal murmured softly, his lips brushing her temple very lightly. 'Or like this?'

His mouth moved to her cheek, his kiss firmer than before, setting a light to the smouldering embers in her heart, making them flare up into burning heat so that she moaned softly, becoming limp in his grasp, her whole body pliant against his hardness. Through the whirling haze that filled her mind she vaguely heard Cal's triumphant laughter deep in his throat.

'Can Joel do this to you, my lovely?' he whispered, trailing searing kisses down her cheek and slowly, tantalisingly, painfully slowly, towards her mouth. 'Can he make you feel this way?'

'No!'

It was a cry of longing, of surrender, as she twisted her head so that her mouth met his in a burning, demanding kiss that released the floodtide of passion she had barely held in check since his mouth had first brushed her forehead, drowning all coherent thought in a boiling sea of feeling that flowed through all her veins so that all she was aware of was Cal, his lips on hers, his hands moving possessively over her body, and the warm scent of him in her nostrils.

'No, Cal, never!' she murmured against his mouth, as her hands slid up around his neck, burying themselves in the golden silk of his hair, pulling his head down towards hers with a strength she hadn't known she possessed.

If there had been any doubt in her mind before, there was none now. Joel's kiss hadn't affected her like this, it hadn't touched her at all. It was Cal that she wanted, Cal that she needed, Cal that she *loved*—and if he wouldn't listen she could tell him with her body, letting him feel the desire that blazed in her heart as she pressed herself closer and closer in response to the clamorous yearning that made her feel she would shatter into tiny pieces if he didn't make love to her here and now.

Impatiently she tugged at his shirt, pulling the buttons free from their fastenings with fingers that were clumsy with need, a sigh of contentment escaping her only when her questing finger-tips touched the smooth warmth of his skin beneath the soft material. She heard Cal's swiftly indrawn breath and a bubble of delighted laughter rose in her throat at the thought that at last she had broken through the wall of constraint he had built around himself, at last she had reached through and touched the real Cal, not the cold, hard mask which was all he had let her see since her arrival at the farm. If he wouldn't listen to her, wouldn't let her communicate with him in any other way, then at least she could use this moment to let him know how she felt in the most basic, most primitive and most instinctive way of all.

Cal was drawing her towards the door and she went with him unresistingly, returning his kisses with a fervour that made him groan aloud as he swung her off her feet

and carried her swiftly upstairs. In his room he barely
paused to set her on her feet before his hands, rough and
urgent, were at her waist, pulling the top of her suit loose
from her skirt before they slid in and upwards to cup and
caress her breasts.

'I want you,' he sighed huskily as he lowered her on to
the softness of the bed. 'Dear God, but I want you. Don't
try to stop me, Helen——'

'Stop you?' Helen's eyes looked fearlessly into the
darkness of his. 'Oh Cal, why should I stop you when it's
what I want too? I——'

Her words died under the pressure of his mouth as she
abandoned herself to the ruthlessly sensual domination
of his kiss, her heart leaping in pleasure and anticipation
as his hands caressed her body, smoothing and stroking.
And then they touched her nipples, tormentingly light
and unsatisfying so that she moaned a faint protest, one
that faded on a sigh of intense gratification as his lips
replaced his fingers and she felt their soft tug against her
aching flesh.

A fever of impatience suffused every nerve and she let
her hands wander as freely over his body as Cal's had
over hers, knowing a glow of exultation as she felt his
shuddering response to her touch. She pressed her mouth
against the fierce pulse that beat at the base of his throat,
glorying in the knowledge that he was incapable of
hiding his reaction from her.

Surely now he would see, now he would know! The
heady mixture of desire and the longing to communicate
her love threatened to drive her out of her mind and she
murmured Cal's name like a litany against his heated
skin as he removed her clothes, bringing her arms up
around him as soon as she was naked, sliding her hands

down over his shoulders and back to his narrow waist, holding him tight against her so that her body was crushed beneath the weight of his.

'Helen!' Cal gasped, but fearful that anything he said might break the mood of the moment she closed his mouth with her own, digging her fingers into the hard muscles of his back and arching her body up against his in silent invitation.

The final moment of union was a second of such pure delight that Helen cried Cal's name aloud in joy, then he was moving, strongly, powerfully, taking her with him out of the real world into another realm of blinding ecstasy, until the intensity of her pleasure exploded in her mind in a golden cascade of sensation.

Very, very slowly she floated back to reality. Her body scarcely seemed to belong to her; she was aware of nothing beyond a languorous, sated feeling and the warmth of Cal so close to her, his body still covering hers. She wanted to stay like this for ever, she thought dreamily, wanted this moment to last for the rest of her life. But then Cal made a move to ease away from her and she felt the chill of cool air on her skin and, surfacing from the golden haze that enclosed her, she tightened her arms around him to hold him still.

'No,' she murmured protestingly. 'Not yet.'

'Helen!' Cal's voice held a laugh of exasperation. 'I'm too heavy—I'll crush you.'

He tried to move again, but still she held him close, a sense of desperation giving her the strength she needed.

'Not yet,' she repeated, keeping her eyes firmly shut, not daring to look into his face. She wanted to keep him close a little while longer, to hold the moment of unity suspended in time if she could. If he moved they would once more become two separate people and she wasn't ready to face that yet. With a sigh Cal subsided against her and she thought she felt his lips brush her hair, though the touch was so light she could not be sure.

For a time they were both silent, still held close in each other's arms, as Helen tried to find the mental strength to open her eyes and look into Cal's face. She was desperately afraid of what she might read there, afraid that he hadn't felt the message of love she had been trying to communicate. If she saw nothing but the withdrawal and hostility she had seen in him before, she knew her heart would break.

But the moment could not be put off for ever, and when Cal moved again she made no attempt to stop him but lay feeling lost and bereft, listening to the faint sounds he made as he dressed again, wondering what was in his mind.

'Helen.' Cal's voice was low. 'I think we might be able to talk more rationally if you got dressed.'

His words hurt as much as any rejection could, stabbing straight to her heart with their cold practicality. Lovemaking shouldn't end like this, she thought miserably, not with this abrupt transition from burning passion to cool reason in the space of a few minutes. They should still be in each other's arms, murmuring gentle words to each other, anticipating making love again as they had on that night in her home—was it only four days ago?

Suddenly she felt shiveringly cold and, sitting up, keeping her face averted so that she could not see Cal's expression, she gathered her scattered clothes. Her hands fumbled awkwardly as she pulled them on, still with her head turned away. But even though she could not see

Cal's face she sensed his eyes on her all the time, watching her, and remembering the intensity of that keen green gaze her skin burned where his eyes rested. Perhaps when she was dressed she wouldn't feel so afraid, so painfully vulnerable.

It was a vain hope, she realised when, fully clothed once more, she sank back on to the bed. Nothing could protect her from her feelings, nothing could be a defence against Cal's rejection if that was what was coming. Steeling herself against what she might see she nerved herself to turn and look straight into Cal's face, but his expression gave her no help. The vivid green eyes were hooded and impenetrable, hiding his thoughts from her, and she could read no hint of help or encouragement in the taut muscles of his face. His silence preyed on her nerves. She felt like some small, cornered animal waiting for a predator to spring. If he didn't say something soon she felt her overwrought nerves might snap under the strain.

'Helen——'

'So now you've got your answer.'

Helen and Cal spoke in the same second, their voices chiming together in the still of the night, his low and strangely hesitant, hers taut and shrill with defiance. For a moment they both hesitated in confusion, then Cal frowned darkly and, leaning forward in his seat, demanded, 'What answer?'

'The answer to those questions you were asking.' It was impossible to disguise the pain in her high, sharp voice, she was past concealing anything from him. 'Surely you know now that Joel doesn't—affect me as you do, that his kiss meant nothing. It meant *nothing*, Cal! He was just trying to comfort me.'

Cal's eyes were fixed on her face, sharp as lasers, his gaze searching, probing as if he was trying to reach deep into her mind and read her innermost thoughts.

'And why did you need comforting, Helen?' he asked softly.

If only she could tell what he was thinking. She didn't know how to answer him, but that green gaze was so piercing she felt he would know if she told him anything less than the truth.

'Because I was lonely—and afraid.' Her voice was just a thin thread of sound, but Cal caught it.

'Afraid of what, Helen?' Then, as she shook her head in despair, unable to answer his question, he went on quietly, 'Joel said it was because of me.'

Helen's head came up sharply, her grey eyes widening in shock.

'Joel said—but how? When——?'

'Just before he so tactfully took himself off to bed.' Cal's tone was dry. 'He said he thought we needed to be alone together.'

So Joel had not been deceived by her declaration that there was nothing between her and Cal! This explained his sudden and unexpected departure. Helen felt as if the room was spinning round her, her feet unsteady on the floor. What else had Joel said? To her complete consternation she realised she had spoken the question out loud.

Cal's smile in response was slow and rather rueful.

'He told me I was all kinds of a fool and blind into the bargain if I couldn't see that you'd come here to see me and no one else. He also said that anyone with half a mind could have seen that your heart wasn't in that kiss—that you were thinking of someone else.'

'He said that?' Helen murmured dazedly. 'But
you——'

Her eyes flashed with hurt anger, remembering the
accusations Cal had flung at her.

'I know.' The despondency of Cal's sigh tore at Helen's
heart, quelling her fury in seconds. 'But I couldn't believe
him. I was angry, Helen. Damn it, I was as jealous as
hell!'

Jealous. Just one small word, but it was enough to give
Helen hope. To be jealous you had to feel something first,
and the fact that Cal had admitted his jealousy gave her
the strength to answer when Cal demanded, 'Helen, tell
me the truth, why did you come here?'

'I told you—I wanted to talk to you.'

'About what?'

Helen drew a deep breath. It was now or never.
Ricky's words 'You have to go back if you're ever to go
forwards' sounded in her head, giving her an idea of
where to begin.

'Cal,' she said softly, 'can we go back to the
beginning—to the time you were in my house?'

She caught the flash of wariness in his eyes and her
spirits lifted slightly. He wasn't as harsh and invulner-
able as he wanted to appear. Doctor Jekyll still lingered
under the cold façade of Mr Hyde. Quietly she touched
the heavy cotton bedspread at her side.

'Come and sit here, Cal,' she said, but he shook his
head silently, making her heart twist painfully inside her.

So he wasn't ready to go that far yet, she thought
sadly—but who could blame him? She had hurt him
terribly—but now she had a chance to put things right
and she was going to grasp it with both hands. Folding
her hands in her lap so that Cal wouldn't see how they

trembled, she exerted every ounce of control she possessed on her voice to keep it calm and steady.

'Do you remember that I talked about David—the man who jilted me on our wedding day?'

And now there was no pain in saying those words, only an exquisite, soaring sense of relief that told her she was finally free of the past.

Cal nodded silently, his green eyes watchful. Helen longed to reach out and smooth the lines of tension from his face, bring relaxation to the tautly held muscles of his body, but she knew that the time was not right for that yet. Perhaps when he had heard what she had to say—— The mixture of hope and fear was almost unbearable, so that she had to force herself to go on.

'David was a lecturer at the Poly. I met him when he came into the office looking for a flat, because he had just moved into the area. I went with him to see several places and when he found what he wanted he took me out to dinner to celebrate.'

Pictures were forming in her mind, the stunned look in David's eyes when he had first seen her, the astonishment he had been unable to hide and which she now knew the true reason for, and other images of those early days when she had first come to know and love David, but now she could look at those memories without hurt or anger, seeing them only as part of a past that was gone.

'After that we saw each other nearly every day. He'd been hurt in the past—he told me he'd loved a girl deeply and she'd rejected him, but he said it was all over, he'd put it behind him, and I—I believed him.'

For the first time Helen's voice faltered. She had truly believed David when he had said that his broken love affair was all in the past, had believed that he was ready to start again, and so she had given her heart, had given all of herself in the confident expectation that her love was returned.

Cal hadn't moved, he might not have been in the room, he was so still and silent, but his eyes had never left her face, and Helen knew that at last he was really listening to her.

'David asked me to marry him and I said yes. I was so happy. I loved him, Cal, and I thought he loved me.'

Helen turned to look deep into Cal's eyes and for a second she thought she saw some spark of feeling, sympathy perhaps, burning in their green depths. Her throat felt dry and she had to swallow hard to relieve it. How long could she go on without some response, some sign from him? But she had to go on, this was what she had come here to say and she couldn't turn back now.

'The wedding was to have been in May last year. Everything was ready—the dress, the presents, the reception. Then on the morning of our wedding day I was just about to go and get changed when a telegram arrived, and later there was a letter explaining everything.'

Helen lowered her eyes to her clasped hands, seeing the whiteness of her knuckles as she clenched them even tighter to retain her control.

'David said that he couldn't go through with the wedding. It wasn't me he wanted to marry at all, it was his former, his lost love. He had been drawn to me because I was the exact double of the girl who had jilted him and he'd deceived himself into believing that I could take her place. He'd been living a lie all that time; he didn't love me, he never had.' Her voice rose sharply. 'He mistook me for someone else, he made love to me thinking I was someone else—he tried to make me into her.'

And now it was all out, the full truth which she had never told anyone before, not even her mother. She hadn't been able to bear to admit that David had used her as a substitute for the girl he had loved, but now she had faced up to the truth and there was an intense relief in having it all out in the open so that her body sagged in relief with the sudden release from the tension that had held her stiff for so long. She felt clean, refreshed, purged of the bitterness and hurt at last.

Cal moved at last, thrusting one hand through the golden silk of his hair, ruffling its bright sleekness.

'Yeah,' he said sardonically. 'I know the feeling.'

Helen shivered inside at his tone. She wasn't over the worst yet. The pain and the hostility were still there, but at least he had responded and the black humour of his remark showed that she had found a chink in his armour, if only the very tiniest one. She had to press home her small advantage while he was still open to her.

'After David I didn't want to know about men—no one ever got near me—until you.'

That brought Cal's head swinging round, the green eyes so raw with shock that Helen's breath caught painfully in her throat, making her next words come out on a shaken gasp.

'I was attracted to you from the start, but I tried to fight it, to hide it. You were right when you told me I was just making a mess of my life, I was trying to deny things I really wanted. But when I found I couldn't fight it any longer I told myself it would be all right if it was just an affair—a brief encounter. I thought I didn't want anything else. Loving David had brought such pain and

disillusionment and I didn't want to go through that
again. But things moved much more quickly than I—
than either of us had anticipated and then——'

'And then I blundered in with both feet telling you that
I loved you.'

Cal's tone had changed perceptibly, he had even taken
a step towards her. Helen's heart leapt with hope, but
ruthlessly she squashed the feeling down again, fearful
that she had felt it too soon. She wasn't out of the
woods yet; one false move could send him back behind
that wall of hostility. She found she was trembling all
over and it was an effort to keep her voice steady as she
continued.

'I panicked,' she admitted honestly. 'I wasn't ready for
anything like that. It seemed——' she lifted her hands in
a small, helpless gesture '—frightening, threatening—it
upset the safe world I thought I'd built after David left
me. I couldn't believe you meant it, and I didn't want to
go through all that again.'

She looked up at Cal as he towered over her, so near
and yet still so very far away, her eyes pleading with him
to believe her, to understand.

'I wasn't thinking straight, and when I said those
things it wasn't you I was hitting out against, it was
David. You released all the anger and the pain I'd
wanted to express to him but had kept hidden inside me
and all I wanted was for you to go away and leave me in
peace. I thought that then things would go back to how
they were before—but that was before I knew how I
really felt about you.'

Cal drew a long, unsteady breath as her voice faded.
Only now did Helen become aware of how his hands had
clenched into tight fists at his side, the small gesture

sharply revealing his inner tension.

'And now?' he asked slowly, his voice husky. 'Do you know how you feel now?'

'Oh, yes.' It came out on a sigh. 'From the moment you left I knew I'd made a mistake, though I tried to pretend it wasn't true. But Ricky guessed that something was wrong. He made me tell him everything and then he helped me see how wrong I'd been, how I'd been pushing all the feelings David had left me with on to you.' Her smile was slightly lop-sided, apologetic. 'I might have come to realise my mistakes on my own, in time, but not quite so soon. It's thanks to Ricky that I'm here now.'

Cal closed his eyes briefly.

'Thank God for brothers,' he murmured fervently, then a second later he was very close to her, bending down so that his face was only inches away from hers. 'Can you tell me how you feel, Helen?' he asked urgently.

'Of course,' she smiled up at him, allowing herself to hope at last, because the raw emotion, the need that had sounded in his voice had told her that the wall he had built around himself was crumbling fast. 'But I think you can guess.'

The change in Cal's face was so sudden, so dramatic that she caught her breath in shock at the sight of it. It was as if the mask that covered his face had suddenly melted, Mr Hyde vanishing for ever, leaving Doctor Jekyll clear for her to see.

'Are you——' Cal seemed to have difficulty saying the words and his voice was hoarse and unsteady. 'Are you trying to say—Helen——' His patience broke abruptly. 'Do you love me?' he demanded roughly.

'Yes, Cal.' Helen sounded firm and confident, her happiness at being finally able to say the words shining clear in her eyes. 'I love you. I'll admit I wasn't sure when I came here—I only knew that I had to see you again, that I couldn't go on with my life until I had. And I couldn't let you go on thinking I'd meant those terrible things I'd said to you on the day you left. Then when I saw you and Joel together I realised that you were somehow special and——'

Just for a second she could not meet Cal's eyes, afraid that what she was about to say might drive him away from her.

'When Joel kissed me it didn't touch me, it was nothing like the way you can make me feel, and it made me so very sure. I knew then that I loved you and—oh, Cal!' Her composure snapped completely. 'You said you loved me and I threw it back in your face, but I was wrong—so terribly wrong and I'm sorry! Can you ever——'

A gentle finger laid across Helen's mouth silenced the tumbling words.

'It's all right,' Cal said softly. 'I said I loved you, and nothing has changed.'

For a long, stunned moment Helen simply stared at him. She had longed so much to hear those words so that now when he had actually spoken them she could hardly believe what she was hearing.

'Nothing——' she choked on the word. 'Cal——'

She couldn't go on, but there was no need to. Cal sensed what she wanted unerringly and with a gentle smile he leaned even closer.

'I love you,' he whispered in her ear, his breath warm against her cheek, but nowhere near as warm as the wave of happiness that surged through her as she took in his words fully for the first time. 'I love you, Helen. I was caught up in your spell from the moment I saw you, and then in the garden, with the moonlight shining on your lovely face, I knew that I'd never met anyone who could compare with you and that I never would again. There is no other woman you remind *me* of. You're unique, my only Helen, the only woman in the world for me.'

There could be no doubt in Helen's mind that Cal's words were true, genuine sincerity rang openly in his voice, telling her that this time there would be no pain, no disillusionment, that this was love for a lifetime, for ever.

The next moment strong hands lifted her from the bed as Cal gathered her up into his arms, pulling her close to him and cradling her face in both his hands, his green eyes locking with her grey ones and holding them with the intensity of his gaze.

'I've been through hell since you threw me out,' he told her roughly. 'I couldn't eat, couldn't sleep—I've been working myself into the ground in an attempt to forget you. But I couldn't forget you.' The raw note in Cal's voice caught on Helen's heart. 'Thinking of you was driving me completely out of my mind. I wanted to go to you—I thought I'd go crazy if I didn't see you again—and then you turn up on my doorstep——'

Cal's laughter was shaken and uneven, his eyes just deep, dark pools in his face.

'I couldn't believe you were real. I thought I was dreaming, hallucinating. But then you seemed so interested in Joel——'

'No!' Helen could not let him finish. 'It was never like that, Cal—*never*! I lied when I said I thought you were Jay Keller—I never wanted him. I only wanted the man I met that night at the party, the man who stayed in my house. His name didn't matter—who or what he was didn't matter—it was only you, Cal, always you!'

She had barely time to finish speaking before Cal was kissing her hungrily like a man who had been starved of physical contact for months rather than a few minutes.

'I love you, Helen,' he murmured against her lips over and over again. 'I love, love, love you.'

Helen could hear the rapid beat of his heart beneath her cheek and her own pulse raced in response as she returned Cal's kisses eagerly, shuddering in delight as his urgent hands moved over her body, setting it alight as only he could. Suddenly Cal's chuckle sounded warmly in her ears.

'Joel will delight in saying "I told you so",' he murmured softly. 'He said that kidnappers often fall in love with their victims. I shall be eternally grateful to him for asking me to take his place that night—if I hadn't you might have kidnapped him as you planned.'

For a second the light left Helen's eyes. What would have happened if there had never been that twist of fate that meant that Cal had taken his brother's place at the last minute? If they had kidnapped Joel as Ricky had originally intended, then she and Cal might never have met and she would never have known this overpowering happiness that she could still scarcely believe was real.

No! She pushed the thought away fiercely. She and Cal would have met somehow, some time. A love like theirs was so wonderful it was inevitable.

'It was meant to be,' she told Cal earnestly. 'Perhaps in one sense we got the wrong man, but in every other he was the right one all the time.'

She saw the brightness of his eyes, the laughter that danced in them, and knew that she had spoken the truth.

Cal was the right man in every way—the right, the only man for her.

'I hope you realise that I intend to turn the tables on you.' Warm humour lifted Cal's voice. 'It's my turn to kidnap you—and I warn you I don't ever intend to let you go.'

Helen looked up into the green eyes that were so deep and dark and loving she felt she might almost drown in them.

'No ransom?' she teased gently.

'None at all,' Cal declared adamantly. 'The only way you're going to get out of this house again is by agreeing to become my wife.'

A delighted smile curved Helen's soft lips and her happiness shone in her eyes.

'I think I might just be able to manage that,' she told him softly.

'You better had,' he growled in mock threat. 'Because, believe me, it's the only way you're going to get your freedom.'

'I don't want my freedon,' Helen assured him with all the sincerity of which she was capable as she pressed herself closer to the warmth of his body. 'All I want is you.'

She saw the look in his eyes, saw them darken even more with the desire that was already sending red-hot flickers of fire running through her veins, and she lifted her head instinctively.

'On second thoughts,' Cal muttered thickly, 'I can think of another way you can pay your ransom.'

Then his head lowered and he claimed her parted lips possessively.

ATTRACTIVE, SPACE SAVING BOOK RACK

Display your most prized novels on this handsome and sturdy book rack. The hand-rubbed walnut finish will blend into your library decor with quiet elegance, providing a practical organizer for your favorite hard-or soft-covered books.

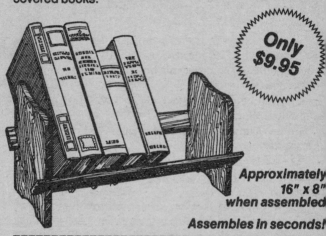

Only $9.95

Approximately 16" x 8" when assembled

Assembles in seconds!

To order, rush your name, address and zip code, along with a check or money order for $10.70* ($9.95 plus 75¢ postage and handling) payable to *Harlequin Reader Service*:

Harlequin Reader Service
Book Rack Offer
901 Fuhrmann Blvd.
P.O. Box 1396
Buffalo, NY 14269-1396

Offer not available in Canada.

*New York and Iowa residents add appropriate sales tax.

BKR-1A

What readers say about Harlequin romance fiction...

"I absolutely adore Harlequin romances!
They are fun and relaxing to read, and
each book provides a wonderful escape."
  —N.E.,* Pacific Palisades, California

"Harlequin is the best in romantic reading."
  —K.G.,* Philadelphia, Pennsylvania

"Harlequins have been my passport to the
world. I have been many places without
ever leaving my doorstep."
  —P.Z.,* Belvedere, Illinois

"My praise for the warmth and adventure
your books bring into my life."
  —D.F.,* Hicksville, New York

"A pleasant way to relax after a busy day."
  —P.W.,* Rector, Arkansas

*Names available on request.

Six exciting series for you every month.. from Harlequin

Harlequin Romance·
The series that started it all

Tender, captivating and heartwarming...
love stories that sweep you off to faraway places
and delight you with the magic of love.

◆

Harlequin Presents·
Powerful contemporary love stories...as individual as the women who read them

The No. 1 romance series...
exciting love stories for you, the woman of today...
a rare blend of passion and dramatic realism.

◆

Harlequin Superromance®
It's more than romance... it's Harlequin Superromance

A sophisticated, contemporary romance-fiction
series, providing you with a longer,
more involving read...a richer mix of complex plots,
realism and adventure.